Ston

A Novel

By

Peter Erskine

Published by Unchained Pen Ltd
∞⋖⬧⋗∞

A CIP catalogue record for this book is available from the
British Library.

ISBN: 978-1-910304-03-7

Stonegate Residents

Year 8:

Staff:

Eleni Fleming
Ben Harrison
Poppy Poynton
Leo Hylton
Alec Tenniel
Amy Tyler
Letty Applegate
Peter "Twig" Beech
Atlanta Greaves
Henry Gray
Kate Juggins
Joe Aston
Sarah Jones
Kirsty Tanner
Jack Parrish
Chloe Shrubb
"Biffo" Swatridge
Adeola Khamisa
David "Dog" O'Grady

Mr Watsham, Headmaster
Mr "Sweaty" Vestey
Mr Kupp, Deputy Head
Mr Kretchner
Mr Cooper
Miss Tina Wilde
Mr Andrew Luxmore, "Mr L"
Mrs Luxmore
Mr "Brocky" Brock
Ms Jenny Peruzzi
Miss Sally Garforth
Mr Attingham, "Batty Attie"
Miss Dalton
Mrs Woznak
Danny

1

Being a murderer myself I suppose that I am best qualified to write this account. If you are the one who fires the gun, who sticks the knife in, who poisons the wine, you have a better right than most to tell the story. You can use blood for ink and not feel guilty. I do not feel guilty – I feel glorious, triumphant, satisfied. Death destroys innocence but broadens the mind wonderfully – I know so much now! But with knowledge comes pain; and I do not think I can stand much more of it. And I feel like dying.

But I must not dwell on my story. I was the flame that lit the fire, but the fire had been laid before I became involved. I should really start with Alec, Leo and Ben, that night outside the staffroom window, and let the whole story tell itself. Without them the whole business may never have come to light at all, and the dead would still be alive, and I wouldn't be sitting here.

Being a murderer.

The dark edifice of Stonegate Hall, boarding and day school for girls and boys aged 3 to 13, stuck grotesquely into the starry, February night sky. At its iron-grey roots angry, moonwashed grass vanished into the darkness of the bleak playing fields while light, like explosions frozen in time escaped from the staffroom windows.

The three, self-appointed Ridicules huddled together in the cold night air, but the entertainment on offer made them impervious to mere temperature. They prided themselves on escapades such as this, and if caught would again be reprimanded for their "ridiculous behaviour" from which phrase they found their name, which they wore as a badge of honour. They jostled each other to get the best view through the window. There was only a thin slit for them to share, but the curtain that fell three inches short of the sill was a protection as well as a hindrance as it prevented light from falling on them from the brightly lit room. The staff could not see them or hear them. The entertainment continued.

There were two people in the room. Miss Wilde, the Form 1 teacher was virtually on top of "Sweaty" Vestey, the tall and muscular Maths teacher. Any closer to him and the first child to have been born at Stonegate for a decade would have been on its way. Miss Wilde, short, curvaceous with a dark, Mediterranean complexion, was the physical opposite of the Teutonic, fair-haired Vestey, who was a favourite with many of the Stonegate mums.

Alec, his eyes as dilated as his wide smile, held his position centre window, half a head taller than the two either side of him.

"Bloody hell! She's going to eat him!" he gasped, his voice wobbling wildly between octaves. As he spoke, Miss Wilde bent forwards as if to whisper in Sweaty's ear and gently bit it. Sweaty's reaction was immediate–he grabbed her thigh with one enormous paw and dived with Dracula like enthusiasm for her neck.

Then Leo sneezed.

It was not a loud, thunderclap of a sneeze but a half suppressed splatter, which sprayed the window and which, much worse, was clearly audible through the thin glass.

The three boys, well practised in methods of escape, scattered into the darkness of the upper playing fields. Alec reacted first. Grinning from fresh memories of the staffroom snogging, he scrambled happily up the fire escape, three steps at a time, thumped into the notice, which stated with total authority EXIT ONLY, crashed into his dorm and was in bed within twenty seconds of the sneeze. Leo hid for two tense minutes by the Theatre which jutted into the shadows near the senior pavilion, content to wait for the right moment before making swiftly for the open library window and locking it, coolly, behind him. And Ben? Ben wasn't running or hiding. Ben was in full view of the staffroom windows if anyone had been watching. He was backing away slowly into the cold air, and he wasn't smiling. He wasn't aware that his arms were crossed tightly across his chest. He continued to stare blankly at the bright staffroom windows. The cautious, monstrous head of Sweaty appeared looking out into the dark night, too blinded by light to see the shivering, emaciated figure standing, ghost-like in the windblown darkness.

And Ben himself did not notice that his pyjama trousers and his slippers were wet and smeared with mud as he turned at last and moved away from the lights of the school buildings towards the darkness of the fields and the hill that led down to the spinney and the river Pendle. Tears wet his cheeks as he sank below the lights of the school but he walked steadily on gazing into the darkness. The ground, surprisingly, became drier as he walked on. Then, when he reached the middle of the lower fields, he stopped abruptly and turned, a minute figure in a vast, dark arena. The school was visible again now except for the lit rooms on the ground floor which were hidden by the shoulder of the hill. The building was gabled, solid, permanent and black. Ben stared at the brooding monolith with a face drained of all expression. The tears on his cheeks dried. The wind whipped in teasing gusts at his thin dressing gown, but Ben did not notice the cold as it slowly stiffened his motionless limbs. He remained frozen in the moment. Then he spoke, quietly. "Someone should sort him," he said. "Damage him," he added.

He turned and walked slowly and mechanically on round the spinney until the school was completely hidden and he was surrounded by blackness. On his left, shrouded by darkness and the tangle of trees, he could dimly make out various tent-like structures clinging to narrow platforms on the steep slope of the spinney. These were the flimsy shelters, made entirely of sticks, moss and other available vegetation, of the Kow Klub, a shadowy and anarchic group of fifth formers and sixth form drop-outs who had "rejected authority, team games, fashion and school food in favour of the real outdoors, story-telling and consumption of smuggled sweets". Their manifesto was for chosen initiates only, and even the rebellious Ben had usually been excluded from their company. He frightened them, and now he passed silently by consumed by his own dark thoughts.

For a brief moment he felt that he was being watched from across the narrow river to his right.

He could make out a stationary human form in the middle of the field. It was leaning at a strange unnatural angle. Then its one, central leg identified it merely as a decrepit scarecrow. Ben relaxed. "Go scare a sparrow," he muttered. "A crow would peck you to pieces." He carried on round the spinney which went in a long curve, following the river bed until, where slope and river met, a path wound up through the trees and then went straight across between two fields back to the school. It was this well trodden path that Ben now followed. In his present mood the dark did not worry him at all, indeed he embraced it with open arms, drank great cold draughts of it, let it chill him body and soul. The routine of many cross-country runs kept him instinctively on the right track and away from brambles and bracken.

As he climbed through the end of the spinney and broke through onto the open fields, some faint starlight glimmered through the broken clouds and dimly lit the path that led back to the school. Ben had welcomed the dark shadows in the spinney, but he felt at one with the stars too, not because they brought light into the blackness, but because he felt a strange sympathy with their isolation and loneliness in the immense emptiness of space. On the level now, he started moving steadily on and soon reached the wet grass of the upper fields and the fire escape, which clung to the sombre walls of the school building. As he climbed wearily up the metal steps, he noticed in the ghostly fire escape lights that mud and water had stained his pyjamas to the knees. Ben felt content that tangible evidence of his secret walk was going to follow him back into the dorm. Matron too would notice it in the morning, but would think better of asking awkward questions. Of Ben anyway.

Break the next morning saw Alec, Leo and several others from Year 8 sprawled casually and carelessly across the Senior Common Room furniture. On the floor were several open ring-binders of various colours displaying mounds of well ordered notes, tests and information sheets: their free time was usually a time to do extra work for their demanding end-of-year exams, but no one was working at the moment – there were things to discuss and everyone was listening.

The atmosphere was warm and close, windows closed against the cold air and the happy playground noises echoing round the grey stone buildings. The bright colours of the Caribbean mural that covered one wall from floor to ceiling helped to dispel the sense of dull monochrome that was trying to seep through the corroded aluminium window frames from outside. The chairs had long since collapsed, and it was possible almost to disappear in their comforting folds. An arm emerged from deep inside the wrecked mounds of a chair.

"Help!" shrieked a muffled voice belonging to the arm. "The Vortex has me. I am slain!"

"Well die then, you maniac, Twig," said Leo with scarcely concealed contempt. Twig's small round, crestfallen face appeared from the Vortex. Poppy giggled, Twig smiled, the others turned and resumed their interrupted conversation.

"They were at it like hamsters," Alec said, grinning. "But you blew it, Leo. They'll retrieve your DNA from the window, and you will be put to death."

"Ha, bloody ha!" retorted Leo.

"Except your snot will mutate and the lab technicians will die within minutes, and we will be the only survivors." Alec was on a runner. He was always a figure to be listened to in these gatherings: he was tall, with hair the colour of burnt corn, and he had a resonant, powerful voice

"Why will *we* survive?" asked Poppy responding brightly to the theme.

"After repeated and prolonged exposure to doses of snot referred to above we have become immune to all known diseases. We will spread out and repopulate the earth."

"Two by two?" asked Twig staring with un-concealed adoration at Poppy.

"No. I shall have a harem and have forty-six children."

Letty casually swept her blond hair from her blue eyes, turned to Alec and raised her eyebrows. "Well, Amy or some other girl will be busy. But you need more than one for a harem," she stated provocatively. Alec, for once nonplussed, gazed at the floor. Letty Applegate – tall, thin and pale, but beautiful in everyone's eyes except her own.

"You could immunize Miss Wilde and take her," said Twig helpfully.

"That tart," said Alec. "No way." There was a sudden serious note to his voice, and everyone in the room focussed on his next, inevitable words. "Those two are a disgrace. Sweaty is married. His wife's a cow, but he's married. And they preach to us in those bloody assemblies about being good. Bloody hypocrites."

"Sweaty's an animal." This from the deep voice of Biffo Swatridge – his first contribution to the discussion. "He's like…" His face distorted with the pain of trying to articulate his thoughts, "…a stag in the butting season." He smiled at the satisfaction this image gave him. The others laughed.

"You mean 'rutting'," said Leo.

"…?" said Biffo. "Whatever."

From her vantage point on the table by the window Letty could gaze down from the Common Room to the playground twenty feet below. A dark-haired, pale-faced, thin figure was slouching, head bowed, hands in pockets, walking slowly and disconsolately towards the door leading to the stairs. The tinies circled in eccentric pattern round him like tadpoles round a grim and determined pike. Ben ignored them. He was after bigger fish.

"Ben's coming," she warned. There was a general readjusting of positions and thoughts as he approached. Only Eleni seemed to welcome the news of his approach without reservation. Momentary silence. Then the sound of feet dragging on stairs. In the room they were quiet. Ben walked round from the stairwell, came slowly in and stopped.

"Who's died then?" Silence. "Or, who, should I ask, is about to die?" The humourless question, which contained more than a touch of real menace, iced the air. Ben was in one of his moods. Which meant that any careless, mistimed word could lead to an outburst of temper. He seemed to gather himself for a second, and then, smiling at Poppy, sat down beside her, put his head back and closed his eyes. The room breathed again. Leo misreading the moment as usual blundered on:

"Yeah, well, we were talking about last -"

Let's get outside," said Ben with decision. "It stinks like the monkey house at Bristol zoo in here." He stood up and, murmuring assent, the others got up too and wandered to the stairwell leaving Twig, stuck happily in his Vortex from the waist down, and Chloe who, completely lost in page 273 of Northern Lights, was perched near the ceiling on a sagging bookshelf and was unaware of the group's conversation or departure from the room.

As the friends emerged into the daylight of the playground the tadpoles and other pond life scattered. Collision with Biffo at any speed other than walking pace was not to be recommended. The group of friends moved, happy in each other's company, towards the grass. The morning frost still muted the greenness and, where the shoulder of the hill dipped towards the lower fields, pale green turned to pure and brilliant white as the sun's rays burst through a gap in the milky clouds and splashed into the children's eyes. The friends, away from the noise of school now, ambled slowly into the sunlight, shoes already wet and shining. They talked and laughed as they moved, talking of things unrelated to school and education. Eleni as usual was looking to the future, a future that she secretly hoped included Ben.

"When I leave here I am going to..." she started, but whatever it was she was going to do they never knew because at that moment the harsh sound of an electric bell interrupted her. As its shrill echoes bounced off the buildings, an equally harsh voice full of irritated authority yelled:

"Get inside, you lot. And don't bring mud into the classroom. Come on, move!" It was the Deputy Head, Mr Kupp, long-faced with his ridiculous goatee beard which, annoyingly, he constantly fiddled with. He turned and strode purposefully towards his office, the central heating, a mug of coffee and his laptop.

"Cupcake has spoken," said Alec. "Let's go."

"What've we got first lesson?" asked Leo, and jumped as a wild girl with pink cheeks and flailing lacrosse racquet ran past, hair and chequered games shirt in disarray.

"Froggish, followed by English!" shrieked Kate, laughing as she disappeared towards the changing rooms. "I'll be late again!" And, as usual, she was.

2

By the second week of term Assembly had already become routine:

"Quiet!" yelled Kupp. "You come into assembly on silence!"

"The mere fact," whispered Joe to Sarah as they sat down, "that he feels that he has to say that proves him wrong." Joe, quick-witted as usual, she thought.

But Sarah smiled at the common sense of this remark, which set the tone for the next ten minutes. If Cupcake was taking the assembly then cynicism and covert whispering were almost compulsory. Although the plush new theatre with its comfortable raked seating had excellent acoustics, it was easier for the children to hear the teacher standing in the well than for him to hear them. Whispering, passing of messages, even minor forms of physical torture were all possible alternatives to actually listening to what was said.

"Stand for the hymn," said Kupp. "'Love divine, all loves excelling'," he added without expression.

The school sang well. Despite the grim introduction, any excuse to lighten the mood with a burst of song was welcome. The pleasant sound even brought a smile to the face of the Headmaster, Mr Watsham, sitting in magnificent authority in the middle of the back row, behind the seniors. As the hymn ended he reverted to his favourite assembly hobby of gazing shiftily with hooded eyes at the provocatively exposed knees of Miss Wilde in the chair next to him.

Three, dirge-like prayers concluded the assembly. Then the short figure of Watsham, "Wet" Watsham, marched in pompous disdain down to the front for announcements: "First fifteen, meet me in break, changed. Don't be late. Dorms 5, 6 and 11, you made an appalling noise last night: off tuck, and early bed tonight. Letty Applegate, please report to my study after lunch." Letty gazed blankly at the strip lighting above her. Quiet, self-effacing and lacking in self-confidence she could not understand why it was always she that was chosen when a "random" child was required by Watsham to answer some spurious question or other. The rest of Year 8 knew why. But the focus was now on Rugby, the 1st XV and the match against St. Peter's, at home. This was the big one, the match that had to be won. Not that Stonegate hadn't already been beaten earlier in the season, in the Christmas term, more than once, but St. Peter's were the local rivals and had to be beaten, on pain of death. According to the Head. Biffo was relishing the encounter too. Lumpish, wide and waddling Biffo transformed into an unstoppable machine when in the centre of a rugby scrum.

"We're going to stuff them!" he said emphatically to Alec as they left the Theatre. Before Alec could riposte with his usual commentary on the pointlessness of quarrelling over a misshapen bouncy ball, Jack, another friendly giant, joined in:

"Their No.8 is going to be mincemeat. I'll wrap him up and send him home in a blood-soaked parcel. He will regret meeting me again."

"Not for long, obviously," said Alec.

"Why not?" asked Biffo.

"He will," sighed Alec gently, "be dead and will therefore cease being able to regret anything."

"Oh," said Biffo, still not understanding.

For once there was a significant crowd watching the match, and although there was quite a bracing wind the sun was out in a clear blue sky.

The rugby season was almost over, and staff, parents and pupils were happy to watch the annual massacre of St. Peter's. The Stonegate captain kicked off and the crowd roared. A brave, red-shirted St. Peter's boy stood square, and caught the ball firmly before being submerged by a sea of green shirted boys, including Biffo and Jack. The ball was won by Stonegate, flung down the line to Sam Benchley on the wing who was tackled and set the ball up for a second-phase attack. This time the stand-off, Toby Watt, saw a gap and sidestepped through, only being stopped five metres short of the line. It was a scrum to Stonegate. Leo put the ball in, stepped to the back row, and flung the ball to Sam on the blind side who zipped over the line and scored in the corner. Try to Stonegate, with two minutes on the clock. History was repeating itself.

And history repeated itself when Ben at fullback got into a fight with a St. Peter's player in an off-the-ball incident and was sent off. Impassive, and impervious to the cold and the admiring glances of the girls on the touchline he stood and watched as St. Peter's were demolished 52-8. Eleni came and stood beside him, smiling shyly from under the hood of her anorak. Ben smiled back, but did not speak.

The coach, Mr Brock, blew the final whistle and gathered the team in a post match huddle.

"Well done, men, that was great. Superb forward play, brilliant, Benchley, on the wing, great effort, Biffo– man of the match again–and really stupid, Ben. Why did you do it?"

"Don't know, Sir, but I didn't like his boots."

"What!"

Jack and several others tittered quietly.

"His boots," with complete equanimity.

"What about his boots?"

"He's a saddo, Sir, he'd polished them."

"So you hit him? No…don't answer. Just go in. You've won the match now go and win the tea." Mr Brock always said that, and Stonegate always did win the tea. Other teams ate like animals, worrying the sausages before chewing them, and eating crumbled chocolate cookies from the palms of their hands.

But at last the St. Peter's team were clambering onto the coach accompanied by three tottering staff, fat bellies bulging a little more than before with the added weight of two pints of beer each had imbibed over post-match analysis in the staff room.

And then free time, and a happy gathering of an exhausted, victorious team and the admiring girls in the Senior Common Room.

"That was good," stated Biffo simply. But any more comment on the massacre was cut short by Henry Gray, gentle, fragile, serious, who had spotted Letty in the corner. She was not looking happy.

"Letty," he said quietly. "What's wrong?" This question was often asked of her. Letty was always ill, or thought she was. If she didn't 'have a bug' her thumb hurt from writing, when her thumb was better she had 'an awful headache'. She looked up. She did not speak, but her thoughts were betrayed by two large

14

tears that welled up in her eyes and rolled down her cheeks. The room silenced. Ben was the first to speak:

"It's that bastard Watsham, isn't it!" he said viciously. "I'll kill him!"

Letty shook her head, still unable to speak.

"I will, I'll..."

"No, you won't." She managed to gasp out the words before burying her head in her hands and weeping uncontrollably. A second's pause before the women took over. Poppy, Amy, Kate and Eleni descended on her and smothered her in hugs and calming words leaving only Chloe, reading on her perch, several concerned but slightly embarrassed boys and one angry, white-faced boy named Ben all wondering what to do next.

Leo broke the deadlock. "Ben, Alec, we need to talk."

"Too right," said Ben bitterly as he got up. Alec also got up and followed the other two Ridicules out of the room without a word. If Alec was silent, something was definitely wrong.

"Ridicules on the warpath." The slightly built and rather verminous Daniel O'Grady, known simply as Dog, always read more into any situation where a good stir could usually get results. It worked this time too.

"Why are they called Ridicules?" asked a small, hesitant voice.

"Because, Master Twig Beech, creature of small intellect and even smaller private parts," said Dog with barely concealed impatience, "they are always being told 'don't be ridiculous' by teachers, so in their rebellious state they decided to call themselves Ridicules rather than Radicals."

"Leave Twig alone," said the imposing and occasionally terrifying Jack.

"What's a Radical?" asked Twig, undaunted.

"A Radical is a revolutionary. It comes from the Latin 'radix' meaning a root. Rather like you, you turnip."

"I warned you," said Jack beginning, unwillingly, to extricate himself from his collapsed upholstery.

"Alright, alright," sighed Dog. "I'm only teasing."

"Well, don't," Jack concluded.

Leo plucked the strings of his prized acoustic guitar gently. The three of them had found a safe haven in the music school, and were ensconced in the warmth of one of the smaller, cosier piano practice rooms. Leo spoke without looking up:

"We have to be careful about this one," he said. It was unusual for Leo, who was impulsively rebellious, to be careful about anything. "We need to think."

"We need to act!" said Ben viciously.

"No we do not, you idiot," said Leo. Although smaller than his two companions his stocky frame and large, deep eyes gave him a presence that compelled people to listen when he spoke.

"Who are you calling..?"

"He's right," said Alec, calmly taking control. "What's the matter with you, Ben? You're not yourself. You've been on the verge of an explosion ever since..."

"...we saw Vestey and Wilde in the staff room," said Leo.

16

"Exactly. What is it, Ben? You are in a bloody awful mood."

Leo twanged out a couple of gentle chords to fill the pregnant silence.

"Are you going to tell us?" Alec asked.

Ben stared long and hard at his two friends.

"No. I can't. You must trust me. Don't worry, I won't lose it. Except against St. Peter's and other punch bags." He suddenly smiled at the memory of his sending-off. And, the tension broken at last, his friends smiled too.

"Do you feel like talking now, Letty?" asked Eleni tentatively. Eleni, with a face like a burst of sunlight and an almost irrepressibly happy and exuberant nature, spoke quietly for once.

"Yes, I do," Letty replied simply.

"Tell us what happened," said the elfin-like Amy.

Park House where the girls' dorms were was away from the main school building, down a rhododendron-lined drive. On the ground floor was the pre-prep, the Acorns. In the day it was a bustling, miniature township with forty-odd tiny people doing their best to be adults before their time. They had a post office, a little shop and pedal cars if they needed to go down the corridor with a message for their Headmistress, who sat in authoritative isolation in her office for as long as she could manage during the working day. But at night-time it was empty, quiet and cold downstairs. The girls' dorms were all upstairs spaced evenly off one long corridor that ran the length of Park House. Robin dorm was situated at the far end of the corridor, far away from house parents and matrons.

17

It was dark and late. The lights had been put out ten minutes before and the feet of authority had disappeared down the corridor. Faint light from orange street lamps glowed gently through the thin curtains like a gentle fire. It was the best possible time for talking, soothing, sorting.

There was a momentary pause as Letty recalled the events of earlier that day.

"I went to the Headmaster's study straight after lunch. He was already there."

"I'll bet he was," whispered Amy. Although smaller than the other girls, Amy's eyes were bright with a fire that could turn to ferocity with the slightest provocation. "Wet" Watsham was a provocation.

Letty paused. "Then he said 'Ah, Letty, good of you to be so prompt'." Her imitation of "Wet's" voice was uncannily accurate, suitably oily. " 'I have the new summer uniform here and I thought you might like a preview,' he continued. He held up that new cotton skirt we've all seen."

"I like it," said Poppy.

"So do I, but that's not the point," warned Amy.

"He got up, came round the desk and held it up to me. He touched me." She visibly flinched at the memory. " 'Just hold it there a moment,' he said, 'while I look.' And then he went back, sat down, and just stared." The tears had started again, but she went on steadily. "He looked at me, not as if…as if…I had the new skirt on, but as if…I had…nothing at all on." Her brows knitted in pain. Her eyes closed. Tears cascaded. "It was horrible. I wanted to…I want to…disappear." Eleni, her bright face now full of pain and concern for her friend, got up, drifted across to Letty and enfolded her in her arms.

18

"We won't let you disappear. We love you. And we are going to beat this." Letty nodded, speechless with emotion.

And Letty, Eleni, Amy and Poppy talked late into the night. And Chloe, who had abandoned her book to the darkness, listened.

Meanwhile, in the boys' dorms up at Main School, a very different scene was being enacted. The dorms at Stonegate Hall were a labyrinth of passages, staircases, secret corners and odd-shaped rooms. They were home to nearly one hundred boys aged eight to thirteen. Up until ten o'clock the matrons and duty staff ruled – running was forbidden, so was fighting, jumping on the beds and so were all the other activities that came naturally to boys who were definitely not ready to go to sleep. Then, at exactly ten o'clock the matrons disappeared into their burrows and the duty staff left the building, locking all doors behind them. Except for the eerie glow of night-lights, darkness infested the whole building. The creaks and groans of a building under stress gradually subsided. Busy washing machines finished their last dizzy cycle of mud-covered rugby shirts and suddenly fell silent. The tired monolith slept. And then the boys came out to play.

Or rather the Year 8 boys came out to play. The juniors were allowed occasional excursions, but only under licence from the seniors and these were only occasionally granted. Tonight was Year 8 playtime and activity was intense.

Twig Beech was short, round and nocturnal. During the day he always hid in corners, away from the light. But at night time he was a different creature. He was first onto the fire escape, first onto the fields and was scuttling down the hill with his small rucksack bouncing on his back. Alec, Henry, Leo, Jack and several others followed, stifling giggles, but pushing and shoving in their eagerness to get down to the spinney fields. They were all dressed in dark green tracksuits which they had put on over pyjamas for purposes of warmth and disguise. By the time they reached the camp fire site, Twig was striking the first match.

"Get more sticks," he ordered. "This lot won't last for five minutes."

"Cool!" said Leo, and loudly vocalized some ascending chords on his imaginary guitar. "Weeow! Weeow! Weeooww!" he caterwauled.

Joe joined in on his invisible drum kit, "Budder, budder, budder, berdang!"

"Where's the food?"

"Who's got the frying-pan?"

"Ou est le bacon!" said Jack, drooling already. "Get the bloody bacon on."

"Ici le bacon et millions of saucissisons!" said Twig in his best French.

Soon there was a fire crackling into life, cleverly confined to a small square arrangement of logs with a sandy base. The huge iron frying pan that was kept in a box by the camp fire was placed carefully on the flames and began sizzling almost as soon as the lumps of butter were dropped in.

"Burn! Burn!" yelled Biffo enthusiastically.

"Where's Ben?" asked Leo.

"And Dog?" added Joe.

"Dog didn't come. He never does. He gets half way then goes back in case he gets caught."

"Weed!"

"Loser!"

20

"Where's Ben?" Leo persisted.

"He was with us," said Alec. "I saw him on the fire escape."

"Well, he's not here."

"Call him."

Leo got up and yelled, "Ben! Where the hell are you, you retard!" No answer, just a faint echo off the far side of the spinney. "Ben!" once more, but again no reply.

"Too bad. More bacon for us," said someone.

"Greedy pig!"

"Yes, I am," agreed someone. And they ate.

Alec was right about Ben. He had come down the fire escape, but had not followed them down to the bottom fields. From the vantage point of the fire escape he had seen a light flickering near the tractor sheds and, putting aside his desire for bacon, had crept off round the outbuildings to investigate. And what he saw brought a grin to his face and set his pulse racing. Without a sound he watched, out of earshot, as two unmistakable figures, one tall and powerful, and the other small, round and cloth-capped, completed their transaction.

"Got him," said Ben, and melted into the darkness of the shadows of Stonegate Hall. But even he did not see, as he climbed silently up the metal fire escape, the small figure of Dog O'Grady gazing at him impassively from the top and disappearing quietly back through into the dorms.

3

Thursday morning started well.

The night had healed bruises, dried tears and poured oil on troubled waters. The unofficial barbecue was still fresh in the memory of the participants, who were all pleasantly tired. The Ridicules and the rest of the Year 8 Scholarship form were preparing in their classroom for the day ahead. They liked their classroom. It was a sanctuary beside but separate from the Senior Common Room which could see up to thirty people crammed into its limited floor space on a winter evening. But in form 6A, the English room, only they, the eleven potential scholars, were allowed occupancy unless special permission was granted. There were only seventeen desks altogether, as the largest form in the senior part of the school never had more than seventeen pupils. The room had little or no children's work on the wall. Instead, it had lines of poetry written in bold italic lines round all four walls. There was some Walt Whitman, William Blake and lines from Elliot's 'Little Gidding'. Prominent above the whiteboard were the words

"And all shall be well and All manner of thing shall be well When the tongues of flame are in-folded into the crowned knot of fire and the fire And the rose are one."

None of the children could say what exactly the words meant but they were comforted by the certainty of their tone, and were content to live with them and accept them. On the opposite wall were a hundred photographs and pictures of faces from all over the world and from various historical eras, all staring out into the room. "Help us!" some seemed to say. Others said "Look at me!" or "Don't look at me!" or simply "Here I am. Who are you?" They were all pictures from beyond the classroom, beyond the confines of Stonegate Hall. And round them the classroom was warm and intimate and, being a first floor room, had views across the fields to the woods where the ugly red sandstone block of Stonegate Manor was hidden tactfully from sight amongst a thick tangle of unkempt conifers a mile away from the school.

And all eleven of them were sitting on chairs or desks or just standing, talking when Mr Luxmore, known simply as Mr L, their form master and English teacher, walked in. Slight of build with dark, thinning hair and a pale complexion he was, in a sport loving school, no one's sporting hero. But his sparkling eyes and mischievous smile spoke of qualities other than the merely physical.

"Hello, Mr L," said Poppy with a happy smile.

"Hello, wunderkinder," he said. He was the one teacher who could address them as "wunderkinder" without there being a trace of sarcasm in his voice. "Please sit." They did so. "You know that all that matters is to love and to be loved, now get your books out, for exams are a necessary evil that temporarily veils this universal truth." Such juxtaposed statements were not unusual for Mr Luxmore. So they got their books out but already knew that there was excitement ahead, controversy, adventure, that they would learn things that they would never forget. They felt that he alone knew them, and in many ways that they knew him. Now in his late fifties he was still enthusiastic about his English teaching. He had an undiminished thirst for knowledge, but more important from their point of view was that they could trust him completely. Most important was that he was more than capable of behaving like a ten-year-old at almost any time.

"Now listen to this. No, do not look at the words, just listen." He bashed the play button of his small but bulbous CD player and the sound of Natasha Bedingfield singing 'These Words' filled the room. 'I love you, I love you, I love you' went the refrain. '…Byron, Shelley and Keats…' she sang. The music stopped.

"Does she know what love is?" was the simple question.

Chloe, well read beyond her years, was first to reply:

"She might do, but the lyrics don't reveal anything. They admit ignorance. She's…trying to be clever by mentioning the Romantic poets, but..."

"...she admits that she doesn't really understand them." Twig, ex-Vortex, beamed from behind his desk, almost hidden except for his round face and raised hand.

"Neither do I," rumbled Jack. And then aware of possible offence added, "I mean they sound good those poems, but I'm not sure I understand what the poets actually felt."

"I agree, Jack," said Mr Luxmore gently. "Let's look at them, and see if we can hear their voices. It's only two hundred years ago, a mere nothing in the history of our damaged Earth. Perhaps their voices are still echoing round the ether. You start, Leo – you even look like Byron, you scruff!"

Leo smiled at the compliment – his hair was as usual unbrushed, his tie at half mast and his shirt untucked - and started, "She walks in beauty like the night…"

Half an hour later they quietly closed their books and listened as Mr Luxmore read them one more poem to complete the picture.

"This is a poem by one Dario Marelli," he said, "who you will not have heard of. It is called, simply, 'Poem for my Love'"

I'm no Byron; he's already said:
"She walks in beauty like the night…"
His images of ideal beauty still
Inspire us with their gentle light.

Words that I can conjure up to show
My love for you, are thin and pale
Beside his powerful eloquence and fire
- the passion that made ladies quail.

Makes no difference to me, for I
Have something that will never dim –
An everlasting love that far outshines
The stars, the universe, and him.

Mr Luxmore put the poem down, and was silent for a moment.

"Does Dario know what love is?" he asked.

"Yes, I think he does," said Poppy.

"I agree," said Mr Luxmore. "Anyway, it's break now. Go and find out for yourselves what love is, and make it quick. I was your age only yesterday and now I'm suddenly fifty-seven. Go!" And laughing, they went.

Mr Luxmore changed the CD, pressed play, sat back and let himself be quietly transported to another world as he listened to the second movement of Chopin's first piano concerto. Not a great poet, Marelli, he thought, but, yes, he does know what love is.

But when they returned after break the mood had changed, and Mr Luxmore knew it.

The garrulous Joe Aston was their chosen spokesman today.

"Sir?"

"Yes, Joe, what do you want? Before you speak I should mention that you look terrified. Don't be. Say what you want, provided that it is not obscene and not in Chinese." Joe relaxed visibly, his shoulders dropped and he spoke:

"Sir, we have some problems." He stopped, not sure how to proceed.

"Just speak, Joe." Mr Luxmore suddenly began to feel weary. The normal easy, carefree atmosphere of the group was tense, expectant. He moved slowly round to the front of his desk, sat on its edge, raised his eyebrows, and waited.

"Sir, it involves the Headmaster." Silence.

"What doesn't," Mr Luxmore said enigmatically. "Carry on."

"Letty is frightened." A further pause. Silence from the whole group especially Letty. Sunlight suddenly flashed across the ceiling, reflected from the windscreen of a passing car outside on the narrow country lane. Joe looked up, straight into Mr Luxmore's worried face. "The Headmaster has been acting inappropriately towards Letty. He touched her. He looked at her…"

"Dirty paedo," said Ben under his breath.

"Shut up, Ben!" said Mr Luxmore, suddenly menacing. "Yes, you especially. You have a wonderful gift for language and you waste it on insult and injury." Then more gently he added, "Well, Joe?"

"It's the third time, Sir. He gets her in his study and..."

"Devours her." This from Kirsty. Everyone was silenced. Kirsty, Head Girl, tough, decisive and widely respected had kept out of the controversy, deliberately walked away from the little whispering gatherings in the Common Room. But when she spoke, everyone listened, including Mr Luxmore.

"Kirsty?"

"He devours her with his hooded eyes, Sir. Whenever he sees her. In the yard, in assembly, in dorm – when he bothers to turn up. It's disgusting. And now he's touched her, gripped her shoulders, touched her hand. What do we do, Sir?"

Mr Luxmore looked across to Letty whose face was once again hidden by her hands. Telltale tears leaked through and dripped onto her skirt. He turned to the others.

"You won't like what I have to say."

"I told you," said Jack bitterly.

"Don't be impertinent!" Mr Luxmore snapped, with such anger and vehemence that the whole class jumped, including Letty.

"Now listen, and listen carefully. You have absolutely no proof of wrongdoing at all. What you have told me amounts to slanderous, idle gossip. You spread any of this any further and you will blight your futures . "

"That doesn't matter," said Ben.

"Yes it bloody well does! What you are saying – especially you, Ben – is dangerous. It is unsubstantiated, uncorroborated gossip. It must stop here."

The form were visibly stunned. Their one hope of help had not only let them down, but also tried to make them feel guilty, as if they were the offenders.

"I hate you!" Without warning, Poppy threw her book to the ground and started for the door, crying hysterically.

"Poppy!" cried Mr Luxmore. But it was too late. She was gone. Leo groaned, muttered, "Girls!" and hid his face in his hands.

Kirsty tried to calm things:

"We thought you, of all people, would listen, Sir. We were wrong. But you have betrayed our trust."

Mr Luxmore looked visibly shaken, more by Kirsty's words than by Poppy's sudden exit from the form room. He raised his hands in a placatory gesture and spoke once more:

"Now, please, please…just listen." There was a sullen silence from the children. Their anger was almost tangible. "What I have just said to you I said because I was frightened of the consequences for you, all of you, if you… crash ahead in the way you are doing. It will rebound on you. You will be silenced. You will lose."

Mr Luxmore paused, closed his eyes several seconds and resumed, talking gently but with directness and sincerity. "What you have just told me makes me weep. We have just been talking about love, and then you confront me suddenly with the opposite - abuse, hatred, and pure evil. If we, in loco parentis, betray you in any way we deserve to burn in Hell.

Remember the quotation 'But whoso causes one of these little ones to stumble, it were better for him that a millstone were hanged about his neck, and that he were drowned in the depth of the sea.'"

Again a silence.

He looked suddenly weary. His voice softened. "You must not say a word to anyone about this. You must stop now. I will do everything within my power to investigate your allegations. There are people I can talk to. If what you allege is the truth, and," Mr Luxmore paused and looked round every face in the form, "if it can be proved to be the truth, then I will carve the stone, put it round his neck and drown him myself." There was a prolonged silence as his words sank in.

"Sir," said Kirsty. "Thank you, Sir." Letty looked up, her face still wet with tears. Already her expression was changing from despair and misery to one more akin to hope.

"Now, for heaven's sake," said Mr Luxmore with a smile, "go and find Poppy and bring her back here. She has a sympathetic and kind nature but is about as emotionally stable as raindrop in a hurricane. I want to talk to her. And you, Letty."

In the weeks that followed, with Mr Luxmore apparently shouldering Letty's burden, things began to get back to normal. There was work to be done, there were exams to prepare for. Even at the weekends there was little time to sit still. There were lessons on Saturday mornings and, as they finished, many children were whisked onto coaches to be taken across the county for matches that had to be won for the honour and continuing good reputation of the school. The children would arrive back at school late in the evening tired, bruised but usually content, with the prospect of some genuine free time to look forward to on Sunday. But even these precious days were invaded by various commitments such as the church service down in the village, letter writing and a compulsory revision session in the evening.

The term sped by. In fits and starts winter changed to spring, the days grew longer and the children began to reclaim the school grounds. Friendships blossomed, strengthened, altered subtly as new, thrilling and terrifying feelings began to stir deep within the children's adolescent frames. Letty continued to feel unwelcome prying eyes upon her but with her friends' support and her trust placed firmly on Mr Luxmore's investigations, she managed to put a brave face on things. Hard work distracted her for much of the time: every teacher claimed that their subject was the most important! Revision was often taken to dorm, by Letty and many others, for secret sessions under the bedclothes by torch light. A sense of unease, though, still gripped her like a living nightmare. But she said nothing, and struggled on from day to day.

4

The end or term was in sight, and with Mr Luxmore taking on responsibility for looking into Letty's complaint, the mood lightened even as the pace of activity increased.

Exams came and went for Year 8, and it was almost as if this hurdle passed was a signal for spring to smash through the frosted ground and invade the air with a million new scents and sounds that were like a potent drug to the children. The "Acorns" from the pre-prep had made headdresses of cut-out early spring flowers and wore them proudly up to lunch in the main school. Even Biffo Swatridge stopped to look as the flower-bedecked crocodile went past laughing and chattering.

The fact that the last two Acorns, Tim Westbury and the minute Peregrine Billington-Potts, decided to break away from the tail of the crocodile and have a fight added to the sense of fun. Peregrine had too many snowdrops and wanted Tim's daffodils and before the figure of Miss Dalton could catch them the yard was littered with cardboard spring flowers ripped up by tiny, angry fists. The front half of the crocodile was already in the double doors that led to the dining-room, but the rear half hearing the noise of the battling boys turned to watch the fight. Tim Westbury had already had enough. His hat was ruined, his face bloody; he stood where he was and howled. But Peregrine had not finished.

Enraged by his cheering classmates he ran at them screaming with fury. They all scattered like blossom in a sudden gust of wind. Their hats and the fragile posies perched on their brims were his target. Like a demented, living scythe he tore into them ripping up two more hats before he could be restrained by shocked but laughing seniors. It took another two minutes for nature to be tamed and order restored. During lunch Adeola Khamisa and Sarah Jones from 6B made four replacement hats of unrivalled excellence and Tim and Peregrine, aged four-and-a-half, learnt that crime most certainly did pay as two angels from nowhere crowned them in floral glory.

Spring was in the air too for Alec who began to neglect his Ridicule threesome for the company of Amy. Normally "pairing-off" was frowned on by the staff as being an activity that only they could openly indulge in, but the two were so obviously just happy to be in each other's company that even the prowling and ever rampant Vestey tolerated the liaison. So besotted was Alec with her that he climbed out of a third floor dorm window, clung to a drainpipe and swung onto the small flat roof of the stairwell in order to retrieve a tennis ball belonging to Amy. She thought her new love was about to die (so did he on the way back) and was so angry she refused to speak to him for a whole day. He won her back by drawing a flower-covered heart on the tennis ball with his and her initials engraved in the centre in green board marker. And by the time of the end of term theatre visit two days later they were again inseparable.

After an early supper the two lovers and the rest of Year 8 scrambled happily onto the coach to Dorchester. They were off to see "Of Mice and Men" which they had all studied that term.

Mr Luxmore looked tired as he climbed on board and started checking names. The expedition did not worry him at all; in fact he was looking forward to it. He knew that the thirty-eight children on the coach and the other two staff, Jenny Peruzzi, the caffeinated art teacher, and Sally Garforth would all love the show. But he was still reeling from two wretched confrontations with colleagues in one day. He hadn't meant to have any rows at all, but he had surprised Mr Kretchner, Letty's personal tutor, in his first floor, bachelor den. Those passing along the corridor opposite and one floor higher had a good view into the room, and had testified that there had been "Lots of gesticerlating" and "lots of noise", partly from Kretchner but mainly from Luxmore. Mr Luxmore had suddenly terminated the interview, gone straight to the useless Kupp ("Cupcake", thought Luxmore suddenly, was a suitably demeaning nickname for the blithering idiot of a Deputy Head), and had had a further unresolved row. Trouble was brewing. Probably for himself.

The only current problem for Mr Luxmore was the less serious matter that, when he had read the last chapter of "Of Mice and Men" to 6B, Kate, who was several chapters behind the rest of the class because of her dyslexia, had burst into uncontrollable tears when George shot Lennie, and she could not be consoled for several hours. The worry was that she would give a repeat performance in the theatre and disrupt the performance. The reality was worse than Mr Luxmore had feared.

"How are you feeling, Kate?" asked Miss Garforth, who had been asked to keep an eye on the troubled girl.

"Fine," said Kate one minute before the performance began. Unfortunately one minute after it began, with George and Lennie within arm's reach of the Stonegate children, Kate's bottom lip began to quiver in anticipation of the inevitable end.

"Pass the tissues!" whispered Miss Garforth. But even a thick wad of tissues was not sound proof and poor Kate was led from the auditorium howling after only five minutes of the play.

At the interval, Mr Luxmore, harassed and worried, was approached by an elderly woman who had witnessed the whole incident.

"Excuse me, but are you in charge of this group of children?"

"Yes, I am, and I am sor..."

"Well, I just wanted to say how moved I was by what happened. Your children obviously appreciate what they are seeing. Charming." And she walked off leaving Mr Luxmore, dazed and confused, thinking that the woman had been about to verbally abuse him. And he only recovered fully when, back on the coach, he realized that Alec and Amy were missing. They were found shortly afterwards sitting hand in hand in the foyer sipping orange juice through two large straws.

"Hello, Sir," said Alec. "Come and have a drink." So he did, and they were all late back to school, but nobody minded.

And all would have been well at the end of term a few days later had it not been for Vestey, Miss Wilde and Mr Kretchner, the alcoholic Head of French, who all decided to have a drinking session in the staff room on the last evening. It was just past 8pm when Vestey burst out of the staff room and collared Henry.

"Henry, come here!"

"Yes, Sir."

"Go and find Ben Harrison and send him here."

"Don't know where he is, Sir."

"Don't be so stupid – that's why I said FIND him, now GO!"

"Yes, Sir." Henry was not happy with his errand. He knew perfectly well where Ben was, but knew equally well that Ben would not want to see Vestey. Ben, for some reason, hated Vestey even more than he hated most of the other teachers. Ben had always been and always would be an enemy of the state.

Henry found Ben in the 6A classroom where he had been all evening with several others. On the last evening of term the friends liked to sit quietly and talk, while the minnows rushed around outside shrieking excitedly, anticipating Easter eggs and their imminent skiing trips to Austria.

"Hi, Ben," said Henry poking his head round the door shyly.

"Hi, Henry," said Eleni. "Come in, join the party."

"Well, thanks, but I can't, actually Sweaty wants Ben, now."

"What!" said Ben. "Are you joking? Tell me you're joking, and if you are I will just thump you once."

"It's not my bloody fault he wants you." Henry, now in the room completely, flinched as the threatening figure of Ben slipped off his desk and advanced towards him. For a second they stood face to face, Henry awaiting his execution timidly.

"Well," said Ben, "are you going to shift your arse or not!"

"Oh…I see…yes," he said, and melted into the doorpost as Ben stormed past.

There was a second's delay before the eight occupants of the room, including Henry, rushed for the window. There was a clear view of the staff room from 6A, and a clear view of Sweaty standing outside, waiting.

"My God! What's happening!" whined Twig.

"Shut up! Listen!" said Leo. "Watch for the fireworks."

But, try as they could, they could not hear what was being said as Ben halted in front of the massive figure of Sweaty. That there was an almighty row going on though was obvious. And despite the fearsome nature of Sweaty in a bad mood, Ben was giving as good as he was getting. And then, suddenly, Ben was flailing wildly at Sweaty with his fists. Sweaty grabbed both Ben's hands, shouting at him to stop, so Ben lashed out with his feet. There was a roar from Sweaty.

"Let's go!" yelled Leo, and the friends rushed for the door as one. But by the time they got to the staff room, Ben and Sweaty and the noise of battle had disappeared. From the staff room the sound of drunken laughter and jaded 70s music continued unabated. Bravely, Kirsty went straight up and knocked on the door. There was no answer so she knocked again, louder, almost battering the door in her anger. Suddenly the door swung open deluging bright light into the darkening yard. Miss Wilde.

"What the Hell do you want! How dare you make that noise!"

"Where is Ben Harrison? Where has Mr Vestey taken him?" Kirsty demanded, standing her ground. In the background there were several members of staff, loaded with drinks and talking loudly while the music thumped off the walls. Mr Kretchner was drinking from a bottle of Champagne and was engaged in chatting up Miss Garforth. Mr Brock, with bulging biceps and skin-tight t-shirt was bellowing with laughter at Mrs Woznak, the Head of Music and her equally humourless husband. Other staff, in various states of drunkenness and stupor littered the tatty chairs. The door closed. Whisperings from behind it. Stifled laughter. Slowly it opened again.

"Your friend Ben, little Benny the bunny," said Miss Wilde with a nasty, intoxicated inflection in her voice, "has been taken to see Mr Watsham. He will be sent home. He is a vicious, rude, wild little beast." She raised her eyebrows, smiled and shut the door.

Kirsty turned to face the others. All of them were in dark shadow now.

"What are we going to do?"

"Bastards!" said Alec.

"Well, thank you for that," said Kirsty. "I repeat, what are we going to do?"

"Save him," said Eleni. "He's my friend."

"You really like him, don't you?" said Poppy innocently.

"Yes, I do. He's having a bad time."

"It's that slut of a mother of his," said Leo.

"You wouldn't say that if he was here."

"No, of course not," Leo replied unabashed, "but he isn't."

But the friends were silent now. They had nothing more to say. The darkness, the shock of Ben's disappearance and the finality of the staff-room door being closed had demoralized them all. They would do something in the morning. In the morning things would be put right. So Eleni, Kirsty, Poppy and Letty said tired goodnights to Henry, Alec, Leo and Twig and they went their separate ways up to dorm.

And when they arrived down at breakfast the next morning, Ben had already gone. It was too late then to do anything. The whirlwind that was the end of term caught them all in its grasp and staff and pupils were whisked off their feet to final assembly, form tidying, staff drinks in the staff room (official this time) and the invasion of monstrous, newly valeted SUVs with their blackened, hostile windows, enormous tyres and, often, tiny occupants. Children were swallowed up, dragging suitcases, gerbils, paintings, half constructed miniature siege machines, tubas, tambourines and trumpets with them. There was hardly time for goodbyes, but Kirsty and Eleni managed to rush back to 6A to have a few urgent words with Mr Luxmore, before he retired, shell-shocked, to his house down by the squash courts.

"Sir," gasped Kirsty, "What happened to Ben?"

"Girls, don't worry about *him*, he's alright. But he did attack Mr Vestey."

"But for a reason," Eleni protested.

"What reason?" Mr Luxmore asked, raising his eyebrows. "No one seems to know, and anyway," he continued before Eleni could speak again, "whatever the reason it was a silly thing to do."

"He was provoked."

"Look, Eleni. Ben has got some problems. I don't know what they are – although I could guess – but to resort to violence will not help him."

"Eleni," said Kirsty, laying a hand on her friend's arm, "Mr L's right, we've got to deal with this sensibly."

"But, girls, aren't we forgetting something?" He paused, gathering his thoughts. "There is a more pressing problem than Ben's early start to the holidays. I don't know quite what to say." Another pause. "Suffice it to say…for the moment, I have been talking to various people about…about Letty…this is very difficult; you must keep this to yourselves…"

"Yes, Sir," the girls said in unison.

"Investigations are ongoing. Things are happening. Girls, I am doing my best. Watch this space. Next term things will be different."

And, by God, they were.

5

There was no sun on the first day of the summer term, but it was warm.

Happy groups of friends spilled into the playground at break time and readjusted their lives. Alec and Amy had already met up, and almost held hands but refrained just in time ("intimate contact of any sort is forbidden": rule book, pg 26, paragraph 3, line 9). They had met twice in the holidays and the relationship was definitely on. Several attempts had been made by members of Year 8 to contact Ben, and it had been established that he had been at home with his dear mum, but had not wanted to talk. And now the friends had gathered in the Common Room, eager to see each other, but all desperate to hear from Ben. And there was definitely a new Ben. He looked confident, at ease, even. "A bit smirky," Poppy remarked to Amy.

A few pleasantries were exchanged waiting for someone to pluck up the courage to ask the vital question. It was Joe who broke the ice:

"Well…?" was all he had to say, looking straight at Ben. The whole room hushed immediately.

"I am happy to announce," he said smiling, "that one large, ugly, ungainly slime-ball called Sweaty…has been well and truly dumped by someone who I am happy once again to call my mum." There was an enormous cheer from the entire gathering even from those who had had no idea that the divorced Mrs

Harrison had been seeing anyone, let alone the married Mr Vestey.

"What on Earth is going on here!" Mr Kupp on the war path, appeared suddenly at the Common Room door and snarled. All eyes were directed at Ben, who smiled easily back at Cupcake. "So you are responsible for this noise are you Ben Harrison? See me in my study at the end of break."

Ben continued to smile beatifically at the Deputy Head.

"With pleasure, dear Cupcake, with pleasure." And before the furious Cupcake could respond, Ben turned and disappeared into his form room with the laughter of his friends ringing in his and Cupcake's ears. Then the bell for the end of break broke the spell and the children began to disperse. 6A gathered in their form room waiting for Mr Luxmore to appear for their first English lesson of the term.

"Anyone seen Mr L?" asked Letty.

"No, I haven't, actually," said Jack.

"Perhaps he's in trouble," said Twig with conspiratorial glee.

"And perhaps you have ceased being an alien in the holidays. Very unlikely but just about possible," said Joe lightly. "He's probably in with Watsham or something. For a moment there was silence in 6A. There was a slight feeling of unease at Mr Luxmore's non-appearance. The form room seemed empty without his enthusiastic and cheerful presence. And the dull light that filled the room, a grey reflection of the blanket of cloud outside the window did not help. There was so much to talk about after the Easter holidays, but for some reason no one felt inclined to talk. Even Alec, the one who could always be trusted to lighten the most sombre of moods, could think of nothing better to do than lift his desk lid and peer at the dormant pile of paper nestling within.

They didn't see Luxmore all morning in fact, and after lunch at the first School Assembly, all optimism, all hope for the term, any feeling that things were getting better evaporated in the course of two minutes.

There was the usual hymn, there were the usual prayers, but there was a tension in the air even before the Headmaster rose to speak.

"I am afraid that at the very start of term, a term which for many will be a great and memorable term, I have to impart some very sad news to you all.

"Mr Luxmore was involved in a serious road accident just up the road from here in the early hours of this morning." There were immediate, incredulous intakes of breath from two hundred mouths; someone sobbed aloud. "He has been taken to the orthopaedic hospital where his condition is said to be critical but stable. Our thoughts are of course with Mrs Luxmore."

There was a loud wail from the back row of pupils. The whole school turned as one. "NO!" It was Letty Applegate and she was standing, holding her hands tight together in front of her. "NO!" she cried again. She stood frozen to the spot for measurable seconds while the school watched in disbelief. And then everything happened at once. Letty barged out of her row and ran from the Theatre crying hysterically. "Miss Peruzzi!" yelled the Headmaster. "Follow her please. Miss Garforth, fetch matron." And then everyone was talking or staring wide-eyed at the action, and duty staff tried in vain to restore order as first the Headmaster and then Mr Kupp turned towards the doors and fled.

Twenty-four hours later, superficially at least, things were back to normal. Lessons had started, Letty was in the Sanatorium at Park House, a light and airy room with flowers on the windowsill and a radio, and the most comfortable bed in the house. She would have twenty-four hours of rest and care.

Mrs Luxmore was at Mr L's bedside. "Critical but stable" meant just that, but the "stable" part meant that Mr Luxmore was in a deep coma. He had life threatening injuries and possible brain damage. Regular bulletins were readily available because several of the Stonegate parents worked at the county hospital, which was only nine miles from the school. Mr Luxmore was lucky, they said, as if he had been any further from a hospital he would never have made it. Mr Luxmore was not lucky, said Leo, as if he had been any nearer to or further from school he wouldn't have been involved in an accident at all. The point was academic. What was undeniable was that 6A and the whole of Year 8 had lost their English teacher, their counsellor, their friend, and the things that were going wrong in their lives were now insoluble.

A reassessment of the friends' position was essential, and the next afternoon saw several of them gather, informally in a small clearing at the far side of the top fields. The grass was quite dry and they sat in a loose circle.

Here was calm, here was quiet.

The gentle wind of late April rustled the myriad silver-green leaves of the tall poplars. A blackbird and a song thrush vied for attention with their beautiful spring songs. Over the lower fields two buzzards wheeled lazily in a thermal created by the warm sandstone outcrops on the far side of the Pendle river. In the distance in the hazy spring sunshine a formation of three blue and yellow helicopters from the training base at Upper Pittsbury quietly buzzed like sleepy bees. The helicopters were always around except in the worst weather and the children now hardly noticed them at all. Being on the upper fields the children were in full view of the school but they, in their turn, could see anyone approaching within two hundred metres. No one, either through tact or through a certain wariness of this powerful band of friends, did approach.

The group talked quietly, content to enjoy the peace of being away from all the gossip and activity that Mr Luxmore's accident had set in motion. Chloe, unusually, was the first to speak out loud. She put her book down carefully on the grass.

"We must go and see Mrs Luxmore," she said decisively.

"We can't bother her," said Amy, "she'll be desperate at the moment."

"Exactly," said Chloe. "That's just why we should go and see her. She needs support not embarrassed people avoiding her. She needs to know that we care, we really care." The friends were silent for a long moment. For most of them sadness and a real sense of loss were affecting them deeply for the first time in their lives.

"Well, not all of us should go. That will be too much. It should just be a few of us." The matronly common sense of Adeola galvanized them. "I shouldn't go; it should be Mr L's form, just a few of you."

"I'd like to go," said Alec.

"Yes, you should," Henry said, "and Leo."

"And Eleni and Kirsty," added Alec. "Anyone else want to go? That's fine then. When shall we go? What shall we take?"

"Flowers," said Poppy. "The daffodils have gone but there are still millions of bluebells down in the spinney. They won't keep long, but they'll be good for a day or two. We can pick some for her. We can pick them now and you can go after tea."

"That's decided then," said Leo as he stood up. "What's he doing, is he mad?" They all turned to look in the direction Leo was pointing. Twig Beech was running towards them, as fast as his short, stout frame let him, and was shouting something and waving his arms in wild circles. The group rose as one. As Twig got closer they began to hear odd words alternating with deep, rasping intakes of breath.

"Danny...Danny...tractor...just crushed it...no chance...no chance at all...," and then he was with them and collapsed onto the grass.

"Leave him," snapped Leo. "Twig, what are you trying to say?" After several more deep breaths Twig turned his still shocked face up to the expectant group.

"Danny," he said. "Danny, the gardener, the groundsman."

"What about him?" Henry asked gently.

"He was in his tractor, last night. On the road. He's the one."

"What are you trying to say? He's what one?" Suddenly Twig became lucid and focused.

"Danny was the one what hit Mr L's car. At free o'clock in the mornin'. He was in the green tractor, the huge one. He hit Mr L, went straight over the top, crushed it flat."

45

"Oh, Jesus Christ!" Amy exclaimed. "Sweet Jesus Christ!"

"Ben's gone wild," Twig continued, with his diction deteriorating as his excitement increased, "been shoutin' about murder, been sayin' it's on purpose. He's had to be locked up. He's bangin' on the door, gone berserk."

"Let's go," said Leo.

"No, wait!" said Poppy. Normally demure and quiet, her suddenly hard tone stopped everyone in their tracks. "haven't you forgotten something? What about Mrs Luxmore? We can't do anything about Ben at the moment; we'll just make it worse. We've got to pick flowers, go and see Mrs Luxmore. That's all, that's all." Her mouth was trembling with suppressed emotion.

"Poppy," said Eleni. "You're right, but I must go to Ben. To see how he is. You take my place. Go to Mrs Luxmore."

"You're both right, for God's sake," said Leo. "Let's do it". Eleni ran off over the field and within ten minutes the others had picked a huge bunch of almost luminous bluebells despite and partly because of rules that stated that they shouldn't, and Poppy proudly carried them as they walked back over the field towards the school.

It was Alec who rang the door bell while Poppy, Kirsty and Leo stayed back at a respectful distance. The Luxmores' garden was still and quiet, an oasis of calm in the middle of a bustling school site. There was little colour so early in the season in the flower beds that led up to the front door but the children's senses were assailed by a glorious scent from a yellow azalea that nestled beside the path. The children secretly hoped that Mrs Luxmore was not at home, but then a faint blue shadow appeared through the frosted glass of the front door, the door slowly opened and a wretched, drawn face looked at them blankly. Mrs Luxmore was older than her husband, already into her 60s. Now, she looked about eighty. Alec was shocked, but had the presence of mind to speak, firmly but quietly.

"Mrs Luxmore, we are very sorry to disturb you. We are from your husband's form, 6A, and we have brought you some flowers. We were desperately sorry to about the accident." Alec was always a good speaker and his tone was reverential but confident and sincere too.

Mrs Luxmore did not move or speak. She stood in the shadow of her door. Her haggard face was grey and blank.

"I'm sorry, Mrs Luxmore. We will just leave the flowers and go."

"No." She spoke with surprising strength. "No, please don't go. Come in, please."

"Mrs Luxmore, we don't want to disturb you."

She opened the door wide. Alec turned to the others, smiled tentatively, turned back to Mrs Luxmore and walked slowly into the house followed silently by the other three. Poppy with a mixture of shyness and pride handed over the flowers, whose scent was already gently invading the porch, and said, "I'm so sorry."

"Thank you, Poppy, for the lovely flowers. Come in and we can talk."

Back at school things had calmed down. The seniors were in prep, half-an-hour's enforced, silent work in the dining-room, and the junior boarders were at Drama Club in the Theatre. Eleni, without a second thought, had come straight off the fields, gone to the Head's office and demanded to see Ben.

"Not a good idea, I think," said Mr Watsham. "Ben's mother has been sent for. He is going home for the foreseeable future."

"Sir, I must see him. He will be alright if he sees me. I will calm him down, wait for his mother with him. Please." The word "please" was not added in a begging tone, but merely as a polite formality. Eleni had not come to negotiate.

Mr Watsham hesitated, then acquiesced:

"Alright, Eleni," he said pompously, as if he was dispensing some gift at his disposal. "You can see him, in the library. You will not be disturbed there for at least half-an-hour. I will bring him to you."

"Thank you, Sir," she said matter-of-factly. She turned on her heel and walked straight to the library.

She pushed open the huge, stripped-oak door, went in and turned on the lights. It was a splendid room the Stonegate library. Originally part of a heavy, Gothic design with a stone arch over a large bay window with a matching fireplace opposite, it had been transformed in the 1980s by a generous gift from a happy parent. The heavy pine and oak panelling had been stripped, the walls painted with a warm pink. The room had been carpeted with light pastel green that toned beautifully with the walls, and magnificent matching curtains hung from all the windows. Handmade, oak-veneered shelving accommodated all the three thousand books of the fiction library. It was about as unlike a normal library as it was possible to be, and was a very popular gathering place for children who had had too much of the school and needed to relax, or simply read in peace.

But this evening, although Eleni loved the room, she felt a distinct sense of unease as she sat down on the voluptuous sofa and waited for Ben. Why had she come to see him? What was she going to say? Why was she going to say it? All she knew was that he had reacted violently to the news of how Mr Luxmore had been hurt; the fact that he was near to death was appalling in itself. Why should Danny's involvement in the accident cause Ben to lose control so completely? These and other questions revolved in her mind for several minutes, and remained unanswered as the door opened and Ben walked quietly in.

"Hello, Eleni," he said.

"Hi, Ben," she replied.

He looked tired, emotionally drained. His eyes were red and damp. He sat down beside her, and slumped back into the soft upholstery. Eleni in contrast stayed perched on the edge.

"How are you feeling?" Eleni asked tentatively.

"Rather shitty actually, and you?" He looked at her, saw the hurt he had caused by his curt comment, and instantly regretted it. "No, I'm sorry, Eleni, I shouldn't have said that."

"That's alright I..."

"No, it's not. You come to see me, risking the wrath of 'Wet', God Almighty Watsham, and I snap at you. Bad start." Both sat silent for a few seconds, uncertain what to say next. But it had to be asked.

"What happened, Ben? What...set you off?"

"I'll tell you, El, I'll tell you. Do you remember at the end of last term when we went for a barbecue down on the bottom fields? Twig organized it."

"Yes, I remember Joe and Jack talking about it."

"Yeah, well. Anyway, I never made it. I wasn't really feeling like it if you want to know the truth. But from the fire escape there's a great view of the back of the school and I could see the tractor sheds, and there was a light coming from them. It was around midnight so I thought it was a bit odd. So I cut the barbecue. Apparently they didn't even notice I wasn't there until the bacon was virtually gone. It was easy not being seen though. I kept in the shadow of Mr L's house and the oak tree in his garden. I looked round the edge of the sheds. There were two figures, their faces lit by a torch. It was that bastard Sweaty, and Danny, with his filthy flat cap. I couldn't hear what they were saying, that only happens in crappy books like the Famous Five. In real life it's always too windy to hear, or you're too far away." He paused for second as he recalled the scene. "Danny handed Sweaty a small package, and Sweaty counted out some notes and gave them to Danny."

"Drugs? Cannabis?"

"Yeah, must have been. What else? So there I was, watching the shit who was having an affair with my mum..."

"Are you sure he was, Ben?"

"Of course I'm bloody sure! Do you want chapter and verse!"

"I didn't mean..."

"Oh, God, I'm sorry. There I go again. El...I'm so sorry."

"It's O.K., Ben. Go on."

"Well, there he was, the big, slobbery bastard, and he was dealing in drugs too. I thought, I even said 'I've got 'im!' But I hadn't, of course. In fact he'd got me. Someone, God knows who, saw me watching him, must've sent a note to Sweaty and told him, and before

50

I could take any action he'd confronted me outside the staff room on the last evening of term. Said Danny had given him the instruction booklet for the gang mower, wrapped in a bit of cloth, ranted about me being out at night, said it wasn't any of my bloody business what he was doing anyway. But, El, I know that wasn't true why give Danny money for a lousy instruction booklet? But it wasn't any good. I, the thick idiot that I am, lost it completely and attacked him. That was all he needed. I was whisked off to Watsham, Mum was summoned and I was home before dawn."

He sighed. There was silence for a moment as Ben reflected and Eleni waited for him to continue. "And what a happy Easter I had. But," he smiled, "blessing in disguise – I lost it with Mum, too. She was furious, but it did the trick. One phone call from behind her bedroom door, and Sweaty was dumped! Bloody great. Mission achieved."

"Yes, Ben, but what's it all got to do with Mr L and the accident?" Ben sat up, suddenly animated.

"Don't you see, Eleni? Mr L said he'd been talking to people."

"Yes, about Letty."

"Yes, but who knows who he'd been talking to? Who knows what he'd found out? You can bet he had been ruffling feathers. Think about it: what was Mr L doing in his car at 3am? And what was Danny doing driving the other way in a tractor at the same time?"

"It might be a coincidence," Eleni offered hopelessly.

"Like bloody hell it is! There are some nasty things going on here, and Mr L found out something, and he's been got rid of." Eleni reacted instantly:

51

"Don't say that! He's not dead! You're just speculating. You don't know if any of this is true. You're just guessing. You just hate Sweaty, and you're guessing." Ben looked at Eleni and shrugged his shoulders. He collapsed back into the cushions.

"I know, El, and, again, I'm sorry. But…you know that Hamlet we've been doing, where it says 'There's something rotten in the state of Denmark'? Eli, there's something rotten at Stonegate Hall too. We've got to do something."

"But what? Our only hope is Mr L and he's in a coma in hospital. It's hopeless."

"Maybe you're right. But, what else is there to do?" Ben seemed to have determination borne of despair as he spoke. "Think of Letty. Think of Mr L. Think of the whole, rotten, bloody set up." Eleni turned to look at Ben.

"Ben, what about *you*?"

"Me?" He sat up and looked at her. "What about me?"

"It's just…with Sweaty and all that – "

"That's over. I said."

"Yes. But what's getting to you then?"

"Getting to me? Nothing." As Ben's tone became more impatient, Eleni stumbled on into unknown territory.

"You keep getting into trouble. You keep snapping at people. At me. What's wrong?" Ben did not answer immediately. He sighed, closed his eyes and seemed to shut himself off from Eleni. "What's wrong?" she asked again. He opened his eyes, looked at her and said coldly:

"What do you care?" Eleni stared at him, hurt, dismayed.

"I care," she said, "more than you know." Shyly and slowly Eleni stretched out her hand, found his and grasped it softly but firmly. "Ben, I want to help you. I know you are going home, but I will wait for you." At these words the anger and bitterness welling up inside him seemed to melt. Her voice reached through the tight knot of darkness inside him. As he looked at Eleni a feeling of immense tenderness towards her welled up in him. This face in front of him, this girl, cared for him, for him! His mother, he knew, had some sort of residual feeling for him although divorce, drink, drugs and desperation to get another man into her life had seriously blunted her maternal instincts. As he looked into the worried eyes of this girl next to him, he began to realize something that he had known subconsciously for a long time, that Eleni was beautiful, that her radiant face and shining eyes were as precious to him as anything, or anybody else in the world.

"Ben," said Eleni gently, "I...care for you and I want to help you." She found it difficult to articulate what she really felt. Thirteen-year-olds were not meant to know what love was. It was an emotion monopolized, guarded jealously by adults. But whatever she was feeling it was real, and suffused her whole body with a warm glow.

And Ben looked back into her eyes, without blinking, without moving, and completely unable to speak.

6

The next day senior lunch was in full swing when Letty drifted into the dining room, sat down at her table and asked for "a big of everything" before anyone could ask her how she was. Since her dramatic exit from assembly two days before she had been one of the main topics of conversation at every level of the school. Even the Acorns were asking awkward questions. "Please, Miss, why did Lettyapplegate run away?" they asked. "I'm sure she didn't, dear," was the totally unsatisfactory but only reply that they received.

"Hi, Letts, how are you?" asked Atlanta.

"Fine, thanks, and it's Letty, not Letts."

"Sorry."

"Don't mention it," Letty replied with a sweet smile, so sweet that it clearly said 'Let's talk about the weather rather than you know what'. Everyone carried on eating their tuna pasta bake, except for Mr Attingham, the Classics master, who sat at the head of the table with a plateful of ham and salad, a perk reserved for the staff; their dietary requirements were obviously different from the children's. Mr Attingham, Batty Attie, was small, with a dark, Mediterranean complexion and sparse, curly hair, and was terrified of children. He had unmistakably autistic tendencies and should never have been teaching at all. With his obsessive love of the minutiae of Latin declensions and conjugations he was at least teaching the subject most suited to his character and condition. The more cruel children used to tease him unmercifully. Jeremy Stinton and Harry Pugsley were giving him Hell.

"Sir," Jeremy began, "I'm most awfully interested in Caesar's first Gallic War." He beamed at Attingham, who stared back terrified by this unwarranted intrusion into his communion with his plate of salad.

"Could you please clarify a moot point for me, Sir, Mr Attingham, Sir?"

"What point?" mumbled Sir, spitting morsels of half digested beetroot onto the table.

"Well, Sir, when Caesar was riding around Gaul, Sir..."

"That's modern France, Sir," added Harry helpfully.

"I know, I know," retorted Mr Attingham brusquely.

"...did he suffer from piles, Sir?"

"I don't know, Stinton, I don't know."

"Piles, or haemorrhoids as they are often called, are a very painful condition I believe, Sir," said Harry with deep concern etched into his face.

Mr Attingham looked from one to the other of his tormentors, his salad forgotten. Leo came to his rescue.

"Knock it off, you two, you dirt-bags, or I'll kick your piles back up your arses."

"Oh, yeah, you and whose army!" snarled Jeremy. Leo replied by merely indicating the eleven other occupants of the double table and saying quietly, "Mine, if you want to know." The tormenting of Mr Attingham ceased abruptly.

Lunch came to an end and, as the children trooped out in silence, the nine survivors of 6A, together with Amy and Henry, sought refuge in the library, which was the seniors' privilege during Rest, during which the entire school read quietly to themselves before afternoon lessons started. As the huge door swung shut noises from the corridor were extinguished abruptly.

"That pasta bake was burnt," said Twig.

"You and your ever empty stomach," laughed Alec.

"He's right, though," said Amy, "it was disgusting."

"I fink," said Twig, brightening visibly, "that it is time for a midnight feast. Behold!" he said dramatically. He walked over to the enormous fireplace, carefully put his fingers in a slit between two strips of panelling and pulled. A section four feet tall by two feet wide came away cleanly and revealed a substantial cavity behind. There was rough stone on either side, and the cavity narrowed and then abruptly stopped. Cobwebs and dust infested the far reaches of the cavity. They all knew about the space behind the fireplace, but they had not known about the mountain of tuck that met their eyes now. Sweets, biscuits, chocolate bars, cans of cola and even a bag of doughnuts were piled up in happy abandon just inside the panel.

"Jesus!" Joe gasped. "Where did that come from? It's enough to feed the five thousand!"

"Mine," said Twig. "Smuggled it in before the start of term and got some more yesterday when Mum went to the second-hand shop. Good in'nit?" The space was not big enough to constitute a passage way or hideaway. It was just a boxed in space that had been left when the thick walls of the school had been completed in the 1860s. The panelling had been worked loose some years before. Generations of children had used it to hide contraband in, but no adults had ever, it seemed, discovered it. It was possible for a small person to hide in it, but cobwebs and cold stone deterred anyone from doing so. Just under two metres high at the entrance, and less than half a metre wide, it tapered steadily until stone met stone in the darkness at the back of the fireplace.

"Nice one, Twig," said Jack, "but isn't it too early in the term for such things? Can't we just scoff some now?"

"Well, yes, you could," agreed Twig. "But I sort of…well…fought that we all needed a bit of a lift, if you see what I mean. Let's have feast – including the girls – here in the library tonight. Then we can talk if you want to at the same time. Work out a modus vivendi."

"A WHAT!" said Amy.

"A way of surviving the term," he explained.

"Well why didn't you say that?" Amy said shaking her head. "Who's invited?"

"The whole of 6A, of course," said Twig. "That goes wivout saying."

"And me!" sang Kate.

"Yes, you, you nutter," said Twig, "and you Amy, and Henry."

"Cool," said Henry, who was more than happy to be included in such an event."

"And Atlanta, even though she's even more crazy than Kate. And Biffo, Adeola, Sarah and Dog."

"Why Dog?" Leo queried. "He's a complete misery. I don't trust him anyway."

"Yeah, I agree, not Dog. Ben can't stand him."

"Ben's not here," Amy said.

"He is in spirit," said Leo.

57

"Right," Twig said. "11:30 tonight. Girls, can you escape alright?"

"Of course," said Kirsty. "Leave the link door open so we can get in the main block."

"Great. That's done. Let's party!"

And it was a memorable gathering. By 11:45pm there were seventeen of them feeding and drinking in the library. They opened the French windows and spilled out onto the steps of the croquet lawn. Well practised in stealth they never made enough noise to be heard by the matrons or by any resident staff like Attingham or Kretchner. Vestey and his ghastly, skeletal wife lived down the drive in Stonegate Cottage. And unless Kupp or Watsham were doing a random night patrol they were safe. Eleni was the only one who missed the party. She arrived as the things were breaking up and she had some news.

"Hi, Eli," said Leo. "We missed you. Where you been?"

"Leo, Letty, Alec. Kirsty. Poppy. Come here, you'll like this." As the small group gathered the rest melted away into the night, knowing sensibly when their time was up. Even Twig, having cleaned up with the help of Jack, Kate and Atlanta disappeared back to dorm via the skip.

"Where you been?" Leo repeated. "God, you're bloody freezing," he said touching her hand.

"Yes, I know. I've been spying. For Ben. I said I'd find things out and I have."

"What?" said Letty eagerly.

"First I went to Sweaty's house," she said. "there wasn't much noise. You know he hates animals as well as children? Well I think all wildlife has been exterminated there – it's all tarmac and stunted shrubs.

It was so still and quiet. But I looked through gaps in the curtains. The place was thick with smoke, and it wasn't ciggies"

"Weed."

"Yes, without a doubt. I could smell it through the gaps in the windows. No double glazing there. Anyway, I was cold and scared – but I wasn't going to get caught. It was just Sweaty and that moaning cow of a wife of his. So I moved on."

"Where to?" asked Poppy.

"Into school. Upstairs."

"In our dorms," said Alec, "you naughty thing."

"You wish," said Eleni with a smile. "No, not near your dorms. I went through the San. You can look down into Mr Kretchner's flat from there. He was at home, and he was busy. He was on the computer and he was angry. Kept getting up and banging the table. I couldn't hear him, but he was swearing, you could tell. And he was drinking, straight from the bottle. And then that tart Wilde came in."

"Woo...oo...ooo..! Here comes the porn!" laughed Alec.

"Grow up, Alec. It's not funny."

"No, it's sexy though!"

"Oh, God! You boys are impossible."

"Shut up, Alec. Go on Eleni," said Letty seriously. Suddenly speech became impossible as a night flight of helicopters flew low past the school. Their headlights momentarily lit the library before they swept quickly away across the countryside. Eleni continued:

"Well, not much more to say. They talked for a few seconds, got a bit closer, then Wilde looked out of the window and so did he."

59

"Did they see you?"

"No way. I was miles away. In the dark. But they were highly visible. So then they shut the blinds. And that was about it."

"So what do you make of it?" asked Letty.

"I don't know. But there's things happening. And we've got to find out what. I'm going to do some more spying."

"Take care, Eleni, for heaven's sake," said Letty. "Remember what's happened to Mr L. There are some nasty people out there. Remember Danny and Sweaty."

"Remember Cupcake," said Leo.

"Why?" asked Alec.

"You're right," Leo replied. "Forget him. I just like saying 'Cupcake'". They all laughed briefly.

"Remember the Headmaster," said Poppy.

"Don't worry, I do," said Eleni.

"So do I," said Letty, "so do I."

The memory of what had happened to Letty and how it still obviously affected her cast a shadow over the group. They were tired too and had lots to think about. The time had come to disperse. But the solemnity of the occasion had got to them, and rather than the normal goodnights, the girls gave the boys brief hugs as well, the natural intimacy of their friendship banishing all thought of the school "no touching" rules, before they disappeared down the drive to Park House. Alec was the last of the boys to move having been momentarily glued to the spot by the extra squeeze that had accompanied Amy's goodbye hug. His night was complete.

7

During Ben's absence, which soon stretched out to two weeks, Eleni grew more and more determined to find out anything that might help his cause.

That several of the staff were rotten to the core had been established beyond any doubt in her mind. Who was not rotten she thought? Miss Garforth was nice, but mousey and weak; she hated confrontation of any sort. Miss Peruzzi was powerful, loud and, basically, friendly, but under all the bonhomie was she to be relied upon? Brocky just hadn't got the brain power to help. He would march in with two left feet forward and fall flat on his face. Mrs Luxmore was wonderful. The children felt comfortable and safe in her presence. Visits to her house by small groups were becoming more common – she welcomed the friends with open arms. But she had her husband to think about and could not be approached on anything controversial. No, she – Eleni – and the others could not count on any adult support within the school.

And the parental route had drawn a blank too. Parents! They loved you and spoilt you but how quickly they could lose touch with you – especially if you were at boarding school for two-thirds of the year from the age of eight. It was the twenty-first century, but the English upper-middle classes still ruled the countryside, and their strictly structured lives were neatly compartmentalized into unbreakable units, boarding school being one of them. In the holidays the children had skiing in Austria, sailing in Cornwall or fishing in Scotland. In term-time the school, in loco parentis, took over, giving parents the freedom to pursue their own interests with promiscuous abandon. Some of the children, in term time, were on their own.

So was this the real reason why children of the rich and famous were sent away to school? Was it to teach them self-reliance, team spirit and independence? Was it to release them from Mummy's apron strings? Or was it in fact the inverse of all these? Did it release the parents from that frightening responsibility that they first faced when a mewling, shrieking baby forced its way into the world? Was, "It's good for you" really a cover for "I've done this for ten years. Enough is enough. It's party time again!"? This was not what Eleni thought. She was close to her parents. And anyway she had not reached the age where she understood cynicism, betrayal, infidelity. She saw with open eyes bad people doing bad things, and she was going to fight them.

And she felt a particular responsibility towards Ben. Yes, she loved him. And she felt protective towards him, not that she would have told him that. His fiercely independent spirit would have run a mile from any hint of pity. But she loved him partly because he *was* so haunted, and desperate and lonely. He had a self-destructive streak in him that she wanted to cure. Thirteen, and in love, she thought! Yes. Yes. Why on earth not?

But what was she to do? Finding proof of any wrongdoing was more difficult than she had thought.

The news from Mrs Luxmore was positive, better every day. Mr L was still in a coma, but his condition had stabilized. For a younger man the injuries he had received would not have been life threatening. But to a fifty-seven year old severe physical trauma could be more than a body could stand, and his condition could deteriorate still, without warning. Mrs L took things from day to day. That he had sustained brain damage was possible but by no means certain. A visit to see him by some of the children was imminent. And an explanation of what he had been doing on the road at 3am was forthcoming from Mrs L.

He had, she told them, decided to change his wall display, having got fed up with the faces staring at him day in, day out. He had spent hours one evening pulling them off the walls. He had worked late into the night but had stopped work in his room at nearly ten to three. Then, still wide awake, he had put his reflector telescope into the car and set off up the hill to look at Venus which happened to be high in the sky at the time – Mr L was a keen if inexperienced amateur astronomer. This much Mrs Luxmore had known even before the accident – Mr L had told her he was going to be working late in his classroom and that he might go up to Shrubb hill afterwards for a bit of star gazing. Danny, it seemed, just happened to be coming the other way having been ploughing at night for the local landowner, Mr Padbury, in order to supplement his meagre income. That was it. Terrible coincidence; bad luck for Mr L. Even worse luck for the truth, Eleni and the friends thought, but for the moment they had to accept it, especially as Mrs Luxmore herself seemed convinced.

Meanwhile, to a certain extent, life went on as normal. The weather held, the leaves sprouted on the trees, the flowers grew in the borders and children laughed and cavorted on the fields with bat, ball and racquet. Brocky and Miss Garforth got the rusting school barbecues out, scrubbed them, rubbed them down, and used them at weekends for the boarders. Some of Year 8 seemed to forget about Ben, and could even be seen chatting in friendly tones to Vestey and Miss Wilde who were often to be seen together in classroom, staff room or on the playing fields.

Dog in particular had always been one to seek the teachers' favour, and the eloquent Joe Aston seemed to enjoy staying behind after lessons for casual chats with "Sir." His parents were both barristers, and adult conversation came naturally to him. The darkly beautiful Sarah would stay behind too, her pursuit of the highly intelligent Joe having nothing to do with his brain and a great deal to do with good looks and designer labels with which he was also endowed in considerable quantities. Joe, happy to have a camp follower, responded by gelling his hair for ten minutes every morning until it resembled the after effects of a lightning strike. When Sarah smiled, the fact that she was at the opposite end of the academic spectrum to Joe disappeared from his thoughts completely.

But the rest of 6A did not forget. They were reminded every day when it came to English of what was wrong. Until a full-time replacement for Mr Luxmore could be found, other teachers had to fill in, and the two teachers who had most free lessons were Mr Kupp and the Headmaster himself. English lessons became a drudge at best and an embarrassing strain at worst. Letty never volunteered an answer when the Head was taking the lesson. He, though, brazenly directed questions at her especially if they involved any reference to beauty or sex. It was as if he could not help himself. Letty burned with indignation and anger.

The others noticed, and sympathized. In 6A the flame of revolution was invisible, but was definitely burning.

When the time came to visit Mr Luxmore, his form drew lots to see who would go. They all volunteered. The three lucky ones were Poppy, Jack and Twig; Mrs L got permission to take them one afternoon during games.

"Be prepared," she told them, "not even to recognize him. He's all wired up with machines and covered still in bandages. His face looks bad too, I'm afraid."

"It's still him though," said Twig solemnly.

"Yes, Twig, it's still him, as always." But they were not prepared for the shock that awaited them in the isolation room where he lay, bathed in spring sunlight. It was a man, in bed; that much was obvious. But that was almost as far as it went. Mr Luxmore was fifty-seven, and despite his permanently pale skin he had been fit and healthy. He had been an active hill walker. But the figure lying here had a sallow, wrinkled complexion. Ugly, purple swellings on his left temple, eyebrow and cheekbone distorted his whole face. Poppy and Twig were visibly upset. Only Jack with his large, open face seemed to be in control.

"Speak to him," said Mrs Luxmore. Poppy hesitated, but then walked slowly forward and bent to within a few inches of her English teacher's damaged face.

"Hello, Mr L, it's me, Poppy. Please get well soon. We miss you...we..." She stopped, having said all she needed to say.

They stayed for half-an-hour, talking to each other but completely aware of the sleeping presence in the bed, then left him with the sun still streaming across the room and shadows from the leaves of the blossom trees outside dancing on the walls.

Jack, Poppy and Twig had to wait until the evening before they could report to the rest of 6A. By then clouds had covered the sky from the west, and a steady drizzle was falling. They met in the library. They tried to keep things matter-of-fact and, for once, succeeded. Their emotional resources had been drained. The friends listened in silence. When they had finished their report Eleni spoke in quiet, measured tones:

"I think he's going to be alright. He may not ever be our teacher again, but I believe he's going to get better. I don't know why, I just do. But someone did this to him, and it wasn't just the wretched Danny. I am going to find out who is responsible and destroy him. Will you all help?"

The statement was dramatic and reminded them all of the situation that they were in. "Of course we will," everyone said at once. Letty put her hand on Eleni's shoulder and said, "You can't do this alone. We are with you."

It was dark outside now as rain clouds swept in from the west and night fell on Stonegate Hall. The tall library windows rattled in the gusts of wind, and rain formed intricate patterns and then small rivulets on the glass. Like tears it seemed; but the time for tears was past. They had to be brave and resourceful. It was going to be a long, restless night for the friends. Did any of them realize what they were taking on? Did any of them doubt their own resolve? The answer to both questions was, No.

But there were other things that demanded their attention too, not the least – work. Some awards had already been won – Chloe, with her fencing and athletics had won a sports award; Alec, multi-talented and characterful had managed to gain an all-rounders award; Kirsty and Letty had won art scholarships in January and Atlanta from the form below had won a music award for her beautiful singing; she was a strange girl, a muddled, voluble philosopher and every waking moment was a crisis, a new theory, a solution to the world's problems. The summer term was the main Scholarship term though and several of 6A were facing the biggest academic challenges of their short lives as they prepared for their May exams to their senior schools. Some of the papers they faced were G.C.S.E standard and were fiercely competitive.

A week of intense revision in which they all helped each other ended, and on the first Sunday in May, Alec, Kirsty, Jack, Joe, Eleni and Twig were collected by various parents and taken off to their prospective senior schools for four days of academic exams and interviews. Leo was the only one who was being examined at Stonegate and was facing a rigorous series of music exams, both practical and theoretical. But for the rest of 6A who were still at the school the week was relaxed and easy. They went down to the Acorns to help look after the tinies. The four and five-year-olds looked upon the older children with wide-eyed admiration, and the older children loved the sweet innocence of the little people. Poppy said that they were away with the fairies and that they were incapable of following a logical pattern of thought.

She loved being with them and soon had them entranced with her stories and her knowledge of the countryside. She was talking to one little group about a

Welsh hill farm and had six of the tiny Acorns sitting cross-legged at her feet. She had a large format book with her, which had panoramic pictures of the Welsh hills. White, fluffy sheep littered the green fields.

"Now," she said slowly and deliberately. "Who can tell me who looks after the sheep?" An enthusiastic hand shot up.

"Yes, Alfie?"

"It's a leopard, Poppy!" Poppy suppressed a laugh.

"I think you mean a *shepherd* not a *leopard*, Alfie," she explained carefully. "A *leopard* is a spotted animal that runs *very* fast." She thought that she had got the message across clearly, but as she continued with her talk another hand shot up.

"Please, Poppy," said a tiny girl called Daisy Hampton. "My cat has spots and sheep run very fast too!"

"Thank you, Daisy," Poppy said before once again continuing with her little talk. The final blow came about half a minute later when Alfie again put his happy hand up and said solemnly:

"'cos sheep run very fast, vat's why vey need a leopard to look after vem." The little group were entirely satisfied with this pronouncement. And so, slowly closing the book, was Poppy.

At three o'clock on their last afternoon with the Acorns Leo, Poppy and Chloe were lazily making their way back up to the school, enjoying the freedom and the sunshine.

"I wouldn't mind being a teacher one day," said Poppy, dreamily.

"Never!" laughed Leo. "The little people are lovely but they're all quite mad. Two and two only makes four when they want it to. I asked Sam – the one with orange hair – how many minutes there were in an hour and he said with absolute confidence and conviction 'two million'. Completely bonkers!"

Letty, who had been saying goodbye to each Acorn separately came running up to join the group.

"Who's for a game of squash?"

"No thanks," said Leo. "I want to veg in the common room."

"And me," said Poppy.

"I'll play," said Chloe who had to be doing something if she wasn't reading. "See you there. Five minutes."

"Four," said Letty, running ahead. "I'll get a ball."

The two girls had a hard-fought game which Chloe won three games to one. It was hot in the squash courts and they were both thirsty and nicely tired, but Letty, competitive as she was, decided to stay for a few minutes. "Catch you up, Chloe, I just want to practise my serve," she said. Chloe wandered happily off to get changed. Letty liked the isolation of the squash courts. They had terrible acoustics and could be deafeningly noisy when there was a good match in progress with an appreciative audience. But when she was by herself she could whisper aloud to the court and hear her own words bounce back to her. She liked the effect this produced of being able to have a conversation with herself, with someone she knew would never be angry with her or tease her. She served the ball. It went high, long and deep, right into the corner. "Bother," she said to herself, "why couldn't I do that earlier?" She smiled to herself. She picked up the ball and tried again. Another perfect serve. Ten more serves and four of them were smack on. Tired but happy she decided to call it a day. "Enough," she whispered. But it was another voice that echoed suddenly from the gallery and shocked her to the core.

"Very good, Letty. Very good." It was the Headmaster, leering from above. How long had he been there, Letty wondered? What had he seen?

"Thank you, Sir," she muttered, heading for the door. Her legs felt like lead. After each step the door seemed to recede into the distance. There was a sound of heavy, quick footsteps on stairs, and before she could even touch the door handle it opened inwards and there was the large, bulky frame of the Headmaster, barring her way.

"It was very good, Letty," he said, "but your grip, you know, it was entirely wrong."

Letty, almost paralysed with fear, forced herself to smile. "Oh, I know, Sir, I'm rubbish! I just play for a bit of fun." Ignoring her remark completely Watsham reached for her racquet, gripped it firmly and said:

"Here, I'll show you." Letty refused to be drawn by his eyes, which she could feel boring into her.

"Oh, no, Sir, don't bother. I've got to be going." But he held on and said with cold authority,

"It's like this, Letty." His hand slid down the racquet until it covered hers. Panic, worse than she had ever known, seized her by the throat. For a second neither of them moved, then a voice called, from outside, and echoed round the squash court, like the voice of an angel. It was Chloe.

"Letty! Telephone! Come quick." And Letty pulled her hand away from that awful grasp and fled into the sunlight. Before the Headmaster could recover Chloe had grabbed Letty roughly by the shoulder and said with urgency: "This way!" and pulled her round the corner of the laundry straight into the ample presence of Miss Peruzzi, besmocked with dripping paint brush in hand. They avoided paint-splattering collision by millimetres.

"Whoa! Whoa! You two. My God, Letty you look as if you've seen an ogre! What a face!"

"She has, Miss Peruzzi! Sorry, gotta go," said Chloe still gripping Letty firmly and attempting to rush past.

"Now wait a second. I was looking for you two anyway."

"But..."

"No 'buts', I want a word." When the fully caffeinated Miss Peruzzi 'wanted a word', she usually meant that she wanted several hundred words, quite often involving brush techniques, bright paint and the Impressionists. That she was entranced by her subject and loud colours everyone knew. She was a living example. The word 'pastel' seldom came into her mind; she always wore blue dungarees, but all her other clothing involved bright, primary colours that spilled out from every available gap like a psychedelic volcano. Her hair had several bright clasps that entirely failed to contain her mass of wild, almost black locks. Each wrist had several coloured bangles that clicked and rattled with every movement; and Miss Peruzzi was always moving.

Letty was forced to contain herself in the face of this voluble and visually mesmerizing assault.

"Come with me." She turned and marched off to the art room with the two girls following in silence. When they arrived they found most of their friends already there. Their exams had finished the day before and they had been dumped unceremoniously back at

71

school. They were not painting but standing around, having been recently corralled by the colourful tornado. There was no time for any chatter.

"You are here," the art teacher yelled, gesticulating theatrically, "because I have been asked to take you wild things on an expedition. The Headmaster thinks that some sort of riot resembling the fall of the Bastille will take place at Stonegate if you embryonic rebels remain within its walls a day longer. Tomorrow is Saturday and I have free lessons because the Acorns will be at home and so we will be going south, into deepest, darkest Dorset and will be climbing to the summit of Eggardon Hill where we will re-enact the last stand of the ancient Britons against the Imperialist Roman legions, recite some Thomas Hardy poetry and have home-made ice cream and honey." She paused in order to breathe. "But I must warn you, before you positively explode with anticipatory excitement, that the Devil himself has been seen at Eggardon, riding across the ramparts on horseback at dusk."

"Cool!" said Jack.

"Fabtastique!" said Twig, still in French mode, and the group spilled out into the sun-filled yard garrulous, happy and exhilarated, their troubles temporarily put aside, if not forgotten.

8

At 8:30 the next morning, the ten adventurers, relaxed and happy in their home clothes were getting ready to board the school minibus.

The day was bright and warm, although even at this early hour large cumulus clouds were massing on the horizon; storms were predicted for later in the day. Miss Peruzzi could be heard approaching from the inner school yard. She was singing an aria from Gotterdammerung in her powerful soprano voice. Even the birds stopped their morning chorus as her voice echoed off the impassive brickwork.

Amy and Henry had come to wave them all off. Their exams were not for several weeks so Saturday morning could only offer them school uniform and normal lessons.

"Bring back some Roman coins," said Amy.

"Or a Celtic skull transfixed by an arrow," said Henry.

"At least bring my I-pod back," Amy said to Leo.

"I will defend it with my life against Romans, Dorset hill-farmers, and sheep," he said with mock heroism. Amy smiled coyly, but before the ever-watchful Twig could react to this a junior boy came rushing up waving a letter.

"Eleni!" he called. "Letter."

"Thanks, Ed," she said. She took the letter eagerly and studied the handwriting on the address. "It's from Ben," she said excitedly.

"Great," said Leo. "Gonna open it?" Eleni hesitated, not sure if the moment was right for reading a letter that could have important news, and maybe some private words for her eyes only.

"No, I'll read it later." The rest had other things on their minds anyway and, as Miss Peruzzi turned the corner, the scramble for seats began.

And they were away before nine o'clock. Jenny did not hang about. She did not like driving but her enthusiasm for getting to the other end of a journey always kept her alert and awake. For the first twenty minutes of the journey she was content to let the excited children chatter away happily. When leaving the school, for any reason, she had a strange sensation that she was being held back by an enormous elastic band, one end of which was tethered to the flagpole at Stonegate, the other end of which was strapped round her waist. She felt it holding her, physically and mentally, and the further she got from the school the more painful this feeling became. The school did not want her to escape she told herself; the outside world was a place of infinite possibility and therefore to be avoided at all costs. Did not the school provide her with all she needed for her wellbeing? She should turn around and go back now, before the pain at her waist became unbearable. Why did she feel the need to escape? The answers to all these questions and more were given her dramatically at a point about twelve miles from Stonegate, when the elastic band suddenly broke and an overwhelming sense of relief and freedom engulfed her.

Freedom! Escape from assembly, bells, meetings, school meals, games, skeletal withered figures in the staff room – they all blew from her mind like chaff from a threshing machine. And she began to sing. She sang songs of triumph and despair, happiness and dejection, from La Traviata, La Boheme, Aida, Carmen - songs from a world where love and hatred fought a continual battle and suffering was frequent and intense; but it was a world unaffected by institutional dullness, boring regulation and tedious routine. She sang, perhaps, a little off key, with the scent-laden wind gusting at her through the open window but her commitment was wonderful to hear; even the music scholar, Atlanta, who had been included in the outing, was impressed, and any children who found it a little hard to take plugged into their I-pods instead. And Jenny's only thought of Stonegate was of a splintered flag-pole with the coils of a huge, broken elastic band wound tightly round its fallen remains.

They walked round Eggardon in order to attack it from the south. It was steeper, more of a challenge from this angle but, as Miss Peruzzi said, "If the Romans managed it with the ancient Britons throwing things at them then we can manage it when they are not". Although it was still before noon it was already warm but no one grumbled as they toiled up the hill towards the ramparts. Even Atlanta who had come wearing flimsy diamante shoes rather than the prescribed trainers soon came under the hill's spell.

There was a stillness and a mystery about this place that they could all feel.

Already the view behind them showed them swathes of wild Dorset countryside, which disappeared into a blue, hazy horizon. Vast cumulonimbus piles of cloud were visible but seemed to remain far away over the hills and the sea that was a dull silver strip on the horizon. The misty distances seemed as if they might at any moment dissolve into nothingness and leave them abandoned on their island hillside. One or two dark shadows hung over the fields closer at hand and spectacular white blooms climbed into the sky above them. But in the gentle summer breeze they were slow moving and the threat seemed subdued and unreal.

The children, in their first rush of energy, moved quickly up the slope of the hill. Soon Joe was on the ridge of the first of three ramparts with Chloe not far behind. He waved to the others and then vanished into the ditch beyond. Chloe, spurred on by his enthusiasm, ran with aching legs straight over into the wide ditch and found Joe standing at the bottom looking up at the next rampart, but not moving and, for once, not talking.

"Hi, Joe," said Chloe cheerfully. But he silenced her with a backward wave of his right arm. Chloe stopped beside him. There was an intense stillness here, out of the breeze away from all noise; even the happy chattering of the rest of the group was inaudible to the two of them as Eggardon began to cast its spell.

"Stop!" hissed Joe from between closed teeth. He was in a semi-crouched position, staring at something on the ground hidden from Chloe's view by Joe's unzipped jacket. "It's incredible...so rare...never seen one before!"

"What?" asked Chloe, wide eyed and inching carefully down the slope towards him. There, balanced delicately on top of a small white flower was a magnificent purple butterfly. Both flower and insect moved gently from side to side in the breeze. Chloe opened her eyes in amazement, but before she could articulate the wonder she felt inside, Joe stood upright, puts his hands casually on his hips, said, "Who gives a damn," and stamped emphatically on both flower and butterfly. The rest of the group witnessed Chloe's hysterical reaction as they came over the first rampart.

"You *murderer*!" she screamed. "You callous, brutal killer! I hate you! Why did you do it!"

"Because," said the calm but amused voice of Jack as he walked slowly up to Chloe, "although that is indeed a Purple Emperor, a rare butterfly that any lepidopterist would love to discover up here, this particular specimen is in fact a plastic one that Joe bought in Poundpincher last week." There were whoops of joy and laughter from all except Chloe. Even Miss Peruzzi laughed. The embarrassed but already smirking Chloe glared at Joe and the second battle of Eggardon hill began as she rushed at him laughing and he failed on purpose to escape.

And a battle they did have as Miss Peruzzi showed them how effective the ramparts must have been two thousand years before. Divided into two groups the children took it in turns to attack each other up the slopes of the three ramparts, and every time they tried, the attackers were repelled with ease by the defenders on top of the highest rampart. During the last assault Poppy slipped and cut her ankle on an exposed piece of chalk. Everyone ran to help as they saw her fall. Poppy hung her head as she bore the pain and her long brown hair covered her face.

"Are you alright, Poppy?" asked Letty. In reply, Poppy looked up, held her hand out and said,

"Look. Real blood!" And seeing the bright red blood glistening on her hand the group were silenced

77

for a moment, and a more sombre mood chilled them all. Miss Peruzzi seized the moment.

"Yes, 6A, real blood. Poppy will survive though. I am sure that some of Eggardon's original inhabitants survived too, but many of them wouldn't have. Many of them probably died here, around you, on these slopes." She gestured slowly but expansively at the hill-fort around them.

"Can we dig for remains?" asked Twig.

"No, you can't. It is a protected site," said Miss Peruzzi. "But, interestingly, the hill has never been excavated properly, and occasionally things are found here, the odd coin or nail, bits of pottery. But, no, you may *not* start your own dig. But you can explore, in pairs or more. After lunch."

The school packed lunches, carried by the children in shared rucksacks had been enlivened with items of smuggled tuck and three large bags of sweets provided by Miss Peruzzi. As the children sat eating and chattering, gazing out over the amazing scenery spread before them school was at last forgotten. Their morning exertions and the anticipation of what was to come filled their minds.

Only Eleni was quiet. The letter from Ben, which she had not yet opened, burned in her pocket. But she was reluctant to read it while at Eggardon in case it had news that would upset the happy equilibrium of the day. She missed Ben; they all missed him, but his disturbed and unhappy demeanour was something to be talked about as a group, together back at school. Not here in the summer sun of a Dorset hillside.

Lunch finished the children split up into pairs to explore Eggardon on their own. They had an hour in which to wander freely, to sit and relax, to drink in the atmosphere of the secret place. Eleni grabbed Atlanta as her partner. She needed someone who, although a little crazy, seemed to be self-assured and afraid of nothing. Atlanta never seemed fazed or intimidated by the world of adults. When shouted at by Cupcake or Vestey or even the Head she would never seem to understand why they were upset. She would wait for the volcano to subside, and would calmly walk away. She once said that her technique involved placing the offending adult in an imagined, pink, soundproof bubble for the duration of the eruption. When a stern voice ended inevitably with the words, "Do you understand!" she would smile politely and reply, "Yes, Sir. Of course, Sir," and quietly walk away. It always worked, she said. But with her friends she was always voluble, intense, alive, and, when required to be so, a great listener.

Eleni and Atlanta wandered slowly, clockwise around the top rampart. Atlanta chattered happily about life, the universe and everything. Among other things she was fascinated by philosophy even though she did not really understand what it was.

"Do you think that we are reincarnations of the original inhabitants of the hill and we have been drawn back here by some invisible force?" She paused for a millesecond to wait for a response and then rushed on. "We could be walking over the remains of our previous selves. This…" she paused to scrape up a meagre handful of white chalk, "…could be where I am buried."

Eleni smiled at her friend, content to wait for the right moment to present itself. Which it did about ten minutes later, when finding a gap in the ramparts they slid down out of the breeze and stretched out in the sun, beside a small windswept gorse bush, and an old piece of wooden fencing that appeared in patches across the hill. Atlanta sensed that Eleni wanted to talk and waited, eybrows raised, for her to speak.

"Atlanta?"

"Yes, Eleni."

Eleni was silent for a few seconds as she struggled to find the right words to express the turmoil going on in her mind. She felt like a spin-drier without a stop button.

"I...I think...something awful's about to happen."

"What? Here? Now?"

Eleni looked up, confused by Atlanta's immediate interruption of her thoughts.

"Sorry," said Atlanta. "I didn't...Just carry on."

Eleni again reflected for a few seconds before speaking again. This time with more resolve.

"It isn't just the teachers being nasty. Not their silly shouting and things, and tests and detentions. It's not even about Letty and that creep Watsham. Something nasty is going on. I know Ben feels it. I don't think he knows what it is, but I am sure that Vestey, and Miss Wilde and may be some of the others are involved."

"Involved in what El?"

A note of frustration crept into Eleni's voice as she answered, "I don't know; that's the point. But there are bad things, evil things going on, and Ben feels it and so do I."

"And so do I," whispered Atlanta.

"What?" exclaimed Eleni. "Really? You feel it too?"

"Of course. We all do, to a certain extent. But couldn't it just be just normal things? You know, booze, boredom, sex, that sort of stuff?"

"No," said Eleni. "It's more than that. I know it is. It's part of the reason why Ben has been sent home, why he's been kept out of the way."

"Well, maybe you're right. But how do you know?"

"I don't. But…well…I've got this letter from Ben. And it's in my pocket, and I think…"

"What?"

"I want to read it now with you, Atlanta." Eleni carefully extracted the crumpled letter from her pocket. It was still sealed tight, and at the top of the envelope was written in red capitals FOR YOUR EYES ONLY. She hesitated for a moment before slowly peeling back the flap, trying not to tear it, whether out of force of habit or growing apprehension about the contents of the letter she herself was unsure. But finally she had the letter in her hands, two closely written sheets in Ben's neat, even slightly flamboyant hand.

"Are you going to read it aloud?" Atlanta asked, trying to keep the tension out of her voice.

"Yes," said Eleni. "I am. But you must…" But what request she was going to make of her Atlanta never knew, because at that moment from round the tight curve of the rampart two iron-age warriors by the names of Jack and Alec, came running at the girls with imaginary swords swinging above their heads.

"Die you Roman whores!" yelled the normally calm Jack as he rushed past with the roaring giant, Alec, close on his heels.

"Oh, shut up! You primitive troglodytes!" returned Atlanta. "Go and hide in a minute cave and suffocate!" But the retort was wasted on the warriors whose momentum had carried them out of sight round the curve of the fort within a few seconds. Eleni, whose grip on the letter had tightened during the

81

attack, slowly unfolded Ben's letter again. But she was again halted in her task, this time by a sudden gust of wind and a darkening of the sky as a cloud raced across the sun. She shivered and noticed that Atlanta too had been distracted by the sudden swirling of the wind. The gorse bush rustled; the loose fence creaked. The atmosphere had changed. The hill, that had seemed so peaceful up until that moment, that had been such a refuge from that other world of school, was suddenly bleaker, more exposed, more powerful than it had been before.

"That was spooky." Atlanta always spoke her thoughts aloud. "Maybe the Devil has come to capture some souls."

"What do you mean?" asked Eleni.

"You know. That story about Eggardon. That every now and then the Devil and his hounds come searching for lost souls to take down to Hell. Peruzzi told us earlier."

"Oh, that's rubbish!"

"No, it's not, El. Cars coming up here at night have lost all power suddenly, people have disappeared or been found mad, wandering around with wild hair and torn clothes. It's true." The hill seemed to be listening because the wind suddenly redoubled its efforts to batter the girls and dislodge them from their place. The ramparts that had afforded them some protection from the wind earlier were now acting like a wind tunnel, and violent gusts whipped at them as the sky darkened further. Atlanta screamed and held her flying hair close to her head. "I don't like this, El. Let's go find the others. I'm frightened.

And then the hail came. It hit them without warning, coming straight down the slope and into their faces. It stung them, and pelted their hands when they tried to cover their faces. Atlanta was whimpering, her normal resilience having evaporated at the first blast of hail.

"Let's run, El! Let's go!" But, incredibly, as she turned to pull Eleni with her she saw her friend get up and start fighting her way up the slope, towards the hail and the dark cloud that now seemed to actually be touching the top of the hill as angry grey wisps of mist and hail whipped round towards them both along the ditch. "El!" Atlanta shouted into the wind. "Come back!" But Eleni either did not hear or was ignoring her. She staggered up the last steep part of the rampart and disappeared over the top leaving the frantic and terrified Atlanta cowering in the ditch beneath. Then, without warning, a hand grabbed at her from behind. She screamed and jerked round. A wild, windblown but friendly face filled her vision. "Alec!" she shouted above the hail and wind. "Thank God it's you! El has just…"

"I know. I saw her," he shouted back. "Where's she gone?"

"I don't know. She just took off."

"Let's go get her then." Alec helped the shivering Atlanta to her feet and set off up the slope pulling her behind him.

"I can't!" she wailed. "My shoes!" Alec looked down and saw her pathetic shoes, flimsy, flat-soled and absolutely useless for going up a wet grassy slope. He hesitated and then he and Atlanta were almost lifted off their feet by a blinding flash of light and a simultaneous crack of thunder that seemed to rip the fabric of the hill apart. Atlanta screamed once, turned tail and fled over the lower rampart, scrambling and slithering over wet grass and rivulets of chalky water. Within a few seconds Alec had caught her up and, almost panicking himself, helped her in her flight away from the monstrous storm.

And then without warning, as they approached a small group of thorn trees on the lower slopes of the hill, they came upon a huddled group of anoraks sheltering in a slight dip in the ground.

"Letty, Leo, Kirsty!" Atlanta wept with relief as she and Alec joined the dripping group.

"Where are the others?" asked Alec.

"S'alright," said Leo's muffled voice emerging from his tangled hood. "They're just down the slope a bit." As he spoke the wind dropped, and the last few wisps of hail scattered on the grass around them. The blackness raced off eastwards and a sudden burst of sunlight splintered off a million drops of rain that covered the chalky grass.

"What about El?" Atlanta wailed. "She's still up there, on top."

"She can't be," said Letty. "She must've come down by now. Who was she with?"

Atlanta was getting frantic. "Me! She was with me! That's the whole point. She left me and went to the top. Then there was that flash and bang, and she was there and we haven't seen her since."

"Jesus Christ!" said Leo. "Let's go find her then. Letty, you take Atlanta to the others. Tell Peruzzi what's happened. Kirsty, Joe, let's go." Exhausted and wet through the three took longer than they wanted ascending the steep flank of the hill. The grass was wet and slippery, and the ramparts had to be climbed at an oblique angle if they were to conquer them at all. They reached the plateau together, but there was no sign of Eleni. Calling her name was difficult as the gusty wind was still blowing strongly towards them.

Twenty minutes after having left the other three they found her. She was not on the top but was sitting cross-legged under a tree on the far side of the hill. She was pale, shivering and bedraggled, but she had a calm almost serene look on her face. She greeted her friends with such a smile that all their worry, anger and frustration at her disappearance evaporated on the spot.

"We were worried, El," said Joe gently. "We were worried, that's all."

"I'm fine," she said. "You see there's no Devil here at all. No hounds, no lost souls. There's nothing to be scared of, not if you face it. There's just us and the wind and rain."

"And about a billion bloody volts of lightning," said Leo.

"Yes," said Eleni quietly, "but it missed me."

"This time it did," added Kirsty solemnly.

Eleni, ignoring the remark, got up, readjusted her soggy clothes and said, "Let's go then." She spoke so calmly that the others who had all been worried and a little frightened were nonplussed. They hardly spoke as the descended the hill carefully and rejoined the rest of the group lower down. Miss was slightly annoyed at perceived misadventures of some of the children.

"I told you to stay in pairs, at least," she stated.

"We did," said Atlanta. "But a stranger dressed in black, with a pack of savage hounds took Eleni off and was about to drag her down to Hades when we arrived and punched him on the nose and we rescued her."

"All right, Atlanta," sighed Miss Peruzzi. "Enough. I won't pursue it this time. Now follow me, all of you. But no strangers dressed in black, please."

Eggardon Hill had done its work. The children would never forget its beauty, its power, its history. They all felt that it had a consciousness all of its own, and that it would retain an inexplicable mystery and majesty forever. They decided that the Thomas Hardy recital could wait for another day – their experiences invited the *writing* of new poetry rather than the recitation of old, however great it was. So, having dried out on the lower slopes of the hill, they happily clambered aboard the mini-bus and went off to have ice-cream with local honey and tea in a village with a funny name somewhere in the middle of Dorset. After tea Miss Peruzzi drove them back to school without operatic accompaniment, and the children, although a little subdued by the thought of what lay ahead, were happy in each other's company and grateful for the escape she had afforded them.

And in Eleni's pocket the letter from Ben, which had escaped the hail, awaited her urgent attention.

9

And later that night Eleni read the letter.

They were all exhausted after their day at Eggardon, but when the lights were turned out at nine-thirty she fought sleep by staring at the ceiling, eyes wide open, and she pinched herself as waves or fatigue threatened to engulf her. There was some quiet talk from several of the girls for about ten minutes. Eleni did not join in though, and one by one the girls dropped off until she was sure she was the only one left awake. There was a slight breeze that occasionally teased the curtains into lazy motion, but the night was silent. Not even Miss Dalton's television, which could often be heard until late from the private side of the boarding house, was on tonight. Eleni waited another twenty minutes before moving. Then she swiftly slipped out of bed, donned her dressing gown and slippers and left the dorm.

The loos were the usual place to go and read or work at night-time, but they were too bright, and there was the risk of visits by inquisitive friends or worse. She ran silently along the carpeted corridor to the very end, turned left, went up a short flight of stairs and slipped quietly into the trunk room. It was the perfect place to find the privacy that she needed. Round behind thirty or so stacked trunks was a small space where the wall was always warm. It retained the heat from the hot water boiler located just the other side of the brickwork. A dim but adequate emergency light illuminated the space more effectively than any torch. She sat on the floor against the wall, extracted the letter from her pocket and opened it. Her hand trembled with anticipation and slight fear as her eyes, getting used to the pale blue light began to read:

Dear Eleni,

Don't know how to start this. So, damn it, I'll just start.

I hate it here with Mum. Just the two of us most of the time. But I can cope with that. As you know, it's a bloody great pile, and I can get lost when I want to or go wander in the fields. Trouble is people keep coming round. Not Vestey – that lowlife is out of it forever. But there are always phone calls, and visitors. And then there are "parties". I am put on display for an hour or so and this hideous pack of luvvies pesters me about "what a naughty boy I am" not being at school. Then they start shrieking with laughter after their second drink of champagne – they always start with that – and start touching me – nothing dirty or anything – just can't leave me alone.

I lost it once: this painted tart, after about half an hour of hair ruffling and so on, said "Give us a kiss little Benny" or something like that and I shook her hand off my shoulder and shouted "You kiss me, you slag, and I'll fucking punch your botoxed lips in!" I knew I'd gone too far – everyone in the room stopped talking – but the bitch just let out a scream of laughter. She loved it. She was still laughing when my dear Mum dragged me up to my room, slammed the door and went back down to join the party.

Bloody hell, Eleni, I've never written this much before, but Mum's nicked my mobile and she's disconnected the main phone.

By the way, better not tell Atlanta or Henry, but their dear parents can't keep away. Because of the coke. Not the drink; the powder, in lines, snuffed up their rotting nostrils. They wait until late for that, but I've seen it through the window, and there are traces on the tables and on the floor the next day before Mary can hoover it up. Load of cokeheads. My Mum too. And here's the sweet little irony, El, I'm not allowed (among other things) to listen to Eminem because it's obscene, but he's the one who said:

"See children, drugs are bahhhd, and if you don't believe him, ask ya mum, She'll tell you how she does 'em all the time. So kids, say no to drugs. Drugs are just bad." Yeah, right.

So now you know why I said FOR YOUR EYES ONLY on the envelope.

And this is private too: I miss you like crazy, Eleni. If you hadn't come to see me in the library that day I was kicked out I don't what I'd have done. I've been able to cling onto that belief that somebody loves me. If you meant it, if you do.

Eleni put the letter down as tears sprang to her eyes. I do mean it, she thought, I do. She held up the sleeve of her dressing gown to her eyes, forced back any further tears, and continued:

But there's something else. What are we going to do? There's Watsham and Letty, there's Vestey, Danny and Luxmore (have you heard any more news about him? I haven't). Not to mention that tart Miss Wilde. Oh, yes – I saw Mr Kretchner in our kitchen the other day. What was he doing here? It wasn't French coaching. Is he supplying the coke? He's a sly one that Kretchner. Keeps himself to himself. We must watch

89

him. I think Mr Luxmore went to see him at the end of last term. any connections - Kretchner, Vestey, Danny? God knows. But we've got to find out, Eleni.

Anyway. This has worn out my writing hand. So I'll end now. Well, Eleni, whatever you feel about me. I love you. Does it sound stupid to say, "I think I always will"? Probably but don't care.

I think I always will.

Love from Ben

*p.s. I forgot. I did say "What are **we** going to do?". I meant **we**. I'm coming back on Friday. See you.*

10

And Friday was the parents meeting for the Year 8 leavers.

The room used was the grand Front Hall, companion room to the library, with the same stripped panelling and warm feel to it. The ceiling was still heavily and darkly varnished and was adorned in gold lettering with the names of Stonegate Hall's illustrious past Headmasters. And among them were some true men of vision, true teachers who – although strict disciplinarians – had built a school where education was still an ideal, something to be cherished. Exams had been of secondary importance.

Some of the Year 8 children had taken their entry exams for their new schools, some had not, but the parents were all eager to grill the staff to see how well the £20,000 annual investment in their progeny had been used. Queues formed at tables, behind which sat the suited and tied teachers, mark books at the ready.

Batty Atty trembled behind a pile of tatty Latin Grammars, waiting for the barbarian, parental assault that each year breached his meagre ramparts and had him back in his bare room an hour later clutching the first of several whiskies. But this was a mere skirmish for the parents, some of whom remembered harassing Batty themselves a generation before when they had been pupils at Stonegate and when, they swore, Atty had been exactly the same age he was now.

Several mothers headed for the preening Head of Mathematics, Vestey, who would spend the evening studying a different set of figures from those in the children's books in front of him. But Mrs Harrison avoided his lascivious stare and wandered purposefully off to interrogate Mr Cooper, the cadaverous, grey-haired Head of History who looked like a blesse de guerre, with a lined and pitted face that had fought many battles in the classroom, if not in the field.

Mrs Harrison sat down, smiled, with a smile that lit up her face as far as the corners of her mouth and not an inch further. "Mr Cooper," she stated.

"Mrs Harrison," replied the Head of History, not as yet intimidated, as war had not yet been declared.

"How *is* Ben's history then?"

Mr Cooper hesitated. With his exaggerated sense of time and date the question seemed irrelevant as Ben had not done any history for several weeks.

"When I last taught him," he started, pausing for careful thought, "Ben's history was progressing as well as could be expected. Under the circumstances," he added unwisely.

"And what circumstances are you referring to?" she fired back.

Still not cowed by this salvo Mr Cooper paused again before continuing:

"The circumstances, Mrs Harrison, of his frequent absences from school and his apparently distracted air when he *is* here." He held up a hand to delay a second salvo. "Mrs Harrison, your son is an excellent historian. He has the ability to write with power and authority when he is so motivated. His use of the *mot juste* has occasionally brought me close to tears. Unfortunately he seems to be preoccupied with a number of issues unrelated to the Hanoverians, with the result that his written work, although well argued and presented, contains opinions and comments not solicited by me and..."

"Mr Cooper!" Mrs Harrison could contain herself no more. "I did not come here to be lectured. I want a simple answer to a simple question. Ben is no longer, for one reason or another, in the scholarship stream. I want to know what grade he will achieve in his 13+ exam, that is all."

"He will without a doubt achieve an A grade."

Mrs Harrison arose abruptly, information received.

"If," continued Mr Cooper, to his interrogator's retreating back, "he actually turns up for the exam."

Meanwhile, the historian in question, Ben was up in his dormitory, unpacking, and fielding cautious but persistent questions from Alec, Joe and Leo.

Alec and Joe were draped over Ben's bed trying and failing to make eye contact with an impassive Ben. Leo was at the far end of the dorm, gently and quietly tuning his guitar, making sure he heard every word of the conversation.

"Why didn't you text or email?" asked Alec tentatively. "We've tried every day for weeks."

"I know."

"We thought you weren't coming back," Alec said.

"Vestey wouldn't say," said Joe.

Ben turned abruptly.

"Why d'you ask *him*?" he asked curling his lip with distaste.

Joe was taken aback.

"Oh, I just bumped into him. Thought I'd ask."

Ben fixed Joe with his eyes for a moment, then turned back to his bag. There was silence for a few seconds before Alec tried another tack.

"Have you heard about Mr Luxmore? He's opened his eyes."

Ben stopped unpacking, but remained with his eyes down.

"Oh, yeah? Said anything has he?"

"No, I don't think so. Some of the girls went to see him again last week. Said he was still looking awful. Mrs L gave them tea and cakes afterwards."

"Always the same ones - the same people, I mean, not the same cakes," said Joe grumpily. "Favouritism."

"Does it matter!" snapped Alec.

"Yes, it does actually," Joe replied.

"No, it...fucking...doesn't!" Ben, eyes still down, spat the words from between clenched teeth.

Leo's guitar fell silent as he looked up, mouth gaping.

"I only said..." began Joe.

"Well only don't say, do you hear!"

"All right, I..." Joe fell silent as Alec gave him a warning stare.

Then a sudden chord from Leo's guitar. The other three turned towards him.

"It seems to me," (another, emphatic chord), "that we have things to talk about," (two more, ascending), "but not until we are all ready, right, Ben?"

"Right, Leo."

"In the meantime," said Leo, smiling and putting his guitar down, "we had great time at Eggardon."

"I heard."

"We fought against Roman ghosts. Then the gods got angry and flung a bolt of lightning at Eleni. They missed."

"On purpose or by mistake?" asked Alec.

"Who knows, dear boy, who knows?"

"I sent her a letter," said Ben, mollified now by Leo's quiet diplomacy.

"I know," said Leo, "We all know. We've been talking about it."

Ben, taken aback, stared incredulously at Leo.

"What do you mean? You can't have...she wouldn't have...!"

"No, no, dear boy," Leo continued with a placatory smile. "You misunderstand. We've all been talking about it simply because no one has read a single word. No one is allowed near it, not me, not the girls, not anyone. What *did* you say?"

Ben did not reply. He looked back at his case.

Quiet, methodical unpacking continued, item by item. A toothbrush, slippers, an iPod – deliberate, calculated placing, item by item on his bedside table. This time, he seemed to be signalling, he had come to stay until the end.

11

Ben's surprise return to Stonegate Hall caused quite a stir the next morning.

Even the cleaners were buzzing with the news and Sylvia and Rose were up in the Year 8 common room half-an-hour earlier than usual to try to see him. They liked him. They said that they always liked "the naughty ones the best", probably because they dared to complain, something that no cleaner ever did if he or she wanted to keep their job. But, to be fair to Sylvia and Rose, they also liked him because even when he was moody, which was almost always, he still managed to say "Good morning" to them, and have a chat about life down in the village. The Headmaster, they knew, did not even know their names let alone where they lived or what family they had. They peered cautiously into the classroom through the wire-laced window and saw Ben and several others sitting and standing in ones and twos getting ready for the day. Normally the start of a new week meant noise and laughter as friends caught up with weekend activity, but today the children were strangely subdued. There was some talk but it was in hushed tones and not audible through the old, time-scarred door. Sylvia and Rose retreated, disappointed, but knew that they could catch up on all the gossip in the lunch queues.

Ben and Eleni were at opposite ends of the room, aware of a certain tension in the air. Ben was gently simmering, knowing that any display of temper so early after his return to school would not be welcomed by anyone, especially Eleni. She, in her turn, looked careworn and tired, but under this fragile surface there was still a steely resolve that controlled her thoughts. There was an invisible fire burning deep within her.

The muted conversation continued for two or three minutes. Eleni sat down and extracted her dog-eared copy of R.M.Ballantyne's Coral Island from her desk. The book was always a comfort to her in times of stress, but this time she was reading one paragraph over and over again without understanding, lost in her thoughts.

A loud thud interrupted quiet as the classroom door was kicked open and a lumbering Jack rolled into the room, arms waving, eyes wide.

"Results are in!" he yelled. "Scholarship results are in. The post. This morning!"

"Oh, God!" said Kirsty, visibly blanching. "I know I've failed. I know it!"

"Rubbish," said Letty, with uncharacteristic force. "If you don't get one no one will."

"Yeah, right," added Kirsty sarcastically. Secretly she knew she would get an award of some sort. A naturally competitive spirit was hoping for the top scholarship though; anything else would be a disappointment.

Then the bell went for assembly and, laughing and chattering as normal, the group of aspiring scholars headed excitedly for the door.

The hymn and prayers past the Headmaster rose to his feet, a smug grin filling his face.

"As many of you may know already I have some exciting news for you all. I am pleased to announce that we have gained a number of major awards in the external Scholarship exams." Awards were always "major" to Watsham. Even a minor bursary awarded to those in abject poverty was given "major" status on the Honours Board in the corridor.

There were excited, expectant whispers round the hall. Watsham held up a hand and silence fell. Revelling in his position of power he hesitated as if he was announcing the results of "Britain's Got Talent".

"First of all, I am pleased to announce that Leo Hylton has won a music scholarship. In his report it was mentioned, and I quote: 'Seldom do we have a candidate who is not only highly proficient at playing his chosen instrument-' in Leo's case of course it is his guitar '-but who is also an accomplished composer'. Very well done, Leo."

There was thunderous applause. Not only were people pleased that Leo had got his scholarship, as he was universally liked by the children, but any legitimate excuse for a riot of any sort was to be welcomed. Again, a raised hand silenced the gathering.

"And there are also major academic awards for..." Again the deliberate hesitation "...Eleni Fleming, Joe Aston, Jack Parrish, Peter Beech and Letty Applegate. Alec Tenniel has been awarded an academic exhibition to go with his all-rounders' award." No applause; a collective intake of breath – what about Kirsty? everyone was thinking. You've forgotten Kirsty. "And lastly..." (smuggest possible grin, accompanied by significant head wobble) "...Kirsty Tanner has won a top scholarship, achieving 100% in her Maths."

Immediate thunderous applause with loud cheering. Above the din Watsham's final comment was almost drowned out:

"A great year for us all at Stonegate Hall."

Cheering, foot stamping, and physical assaults on the successful candidates delivered by all who could reach continued for several seconds. The preening Headmaster left the stage and left the wild scenes of jubilation to Mr Kupp, whose pleasure at knowing of the high grades achieved in his subject, Latin, was matched by a general dislike of children and a particular dislike of children making a noise.

"Enough!" he yelled. "You are," he added as the noise subsided, "already two minutes late for lessons. So I want silence from all of you while you are dismissed." Silence fell except for several staff who continued talking obstinately while Kupp glared at them grimly.

The happy friends wandered back to 6A to collect their books for the first lesson. Eleni, having won a scholarship, was considerably happier and was chattering to Letty. Ben seemed to have come to life too and addressed the whole form, grinning:

"Well done, scholars all," he said, bowing. "I remain your humble servant, being the only member of this elevated group not to have received a gilded laurel crown from the Gods of Stonegate Hall." Unaware of any intended irony or unwilling to believe that Ben could rob them of their moment of glory there was general approval of his comic performance. Alec caught the mood, or thought he had:

"Compliment accepted, o insignificant morsel. Now step aside and let the elite continue with their pursuit of academia!"

The others laughed at this continued performance. Ben smiled with them and added: "Your names, my lords and ladies, will shortly be emblazoned in black on the Honours Board. I am only surprised and a little saddened that none of you has yet received a knighthood." This last word was emphasized just a little too strongly for the hint of sarcasm to be ignored any more. And, of all of them, it was Eleni who spoke first.

"Ben, don't spoil it!" she pleaded. "Sometimes you go too far." Ben, stung immediately by her comment, reacted badly.

"Oh, so sorry to be a party pooper, but surely you saw dearest Mr Watsham revelling in reflected glory, positively glowing with pride in having actually achieved nothing at all."

"Don't...," started Eleni.

"Don't what?" Ben challenged. "Pretend I haven't noticed that he thinks it's *him* that has won all the awards? Pretend that..."

"Ben, for god's sake shut it!" said Alec impatiently.

"Yeah, loser!" added Joe unkindly.

"Joe," Letty protested. But the damage had been done. Ben turned away angrily and hurried off to Geography where their topic of glaciation perfectly reflected his mood throughout the following forty-five minutes.

At break time Ben was, for once, contrite. He had always been a natural leader and part of his skill in being one was knowing when and how to regain lost ground. He was conciliatory and as soon as the others caught the mood there was palpable relief all round the Common Room which was more crowded than usual because of the exam news. In all, twelve bodies were squeezed into chairs and sofas designed for six. Twig, emerging from his vortex was met by two substantial shapes named Biffo and Adeola firmly wedged into the exit of his personal universe. He retreated and emerged from the back of the chair, hair ruffled and a look of barely concealed irritation on his face. "You two are breaking the 'no touching' rule," he said. "In fact you are so close you will probably merge with each other like two lumps of lard."

"Are you calling me fat?" asked Biffo threateningly.

"No," replied Twig. "Just impressively large."

There was silent acknowledgement of this fact by the onlookers.

"Sorry," Ben began, and looked round with a clownish grin. "I was silly earlier. I'm really pleased about all your exams. Absolutely brill. And, yes, I am a loser."

"No, you're not," said Eleni quickly. Then to avoid embarrassment added: "You're a git but not a loser!"

"Well, thanks, Eleni." There was a ripple of laughter round the room and Eleni was embarrassed anyway.

"You've made the grade, you have. Nothing to worry about from those on high."

"I'm not worried by them anyway," said Joe.

The gorgeous Sarah, snuggled down beside her heroic Joe, agreed:

"I like Miss Peruzzi. And Mr Brock. And Mr Cooper; he gave me an A for the last assessment. And Batty Atty."

"...is completely insane," said Kate cheerfully. "I know, because I am too!"

"And Vestey?" said Ben quietly, and with barely concealed contempt added. "Do you fancy him too, Sarah, because I bet he fancies you."

"*I* fancy you," said a forlorn Dog.

"I know you do," said Sarah, "and you're a sweetie. But Vestey doesn't!" she protested. "And you, Ben, are foul for even suggesting that."

"Yes, bug off, Ben," said Joe, irritated.

"O.K., sorry again," said Ben, "but have we all forgotten about Vestey's behaviour, and the Headmaster's? Just a few weeks and you all forget."

"Watch what you say about Watsham," Chloe interjected from her usual bookshelf. "Comments like that get back to him somehow."

"Yeah, so there's a snitch. Probably here right now. Won't stop me speaking my mind. Watsham, you're a paedo!" Ben said aloud.

"Don't be silly," said Eleni disapprovingly.

"What, are you...?"

"No, of course not, but you must be careful. I want you *here*!"

"Wooooooo!" said several voices at once amid laughter and a thump as Biffo's large body finally dislodged Adeola and dumped her ignominiously onto the floor.

Eleni coloured and remained silent.

The end of break was approaching and Adeola's removal from the chair was a signal for the rest to start drifting away. Soon, only Eleni and Ben were left, even Twig and Chloe being tactful enough to leave them in peace.

"Ben?"

"Yes, El."

"I've missed you."

"Me too."

Silence.

"I've been doing stuff. You know. While you've been away."

"Yeah?"

102

"I've been watching Kretchner, and Miss Wilde. And Danny – he's always in the school late. He's the *groundsman*."

"And all the rest," said Ben. "D'you remember when I saw him and Sweaty exchanging stuff?"

"Yes, Ben, but someone saw *you*. You were seen on the fire escape, and whoever saw you told Sweaty. That's why he went for you the next day. That's why you got sent home."

"How do you know all this, El?"

"I heard Sweaty talking to Miss Wilde. He told her you'd been seen there. It's all been locked up now."

"That's illegal – it's a fire escape."

"No, Ben – it's on an automatic system. There's a fire, it opens automatically."

"Vestey...Sweaty. I hate him."

"That's no use. We've got to do something."

"No one's interested," said Ben. "You heard them. Last few weeks of their life here. They don't want to know."

"Well, I do, Ben, and so does Letty, but she's scared. Leo and Alec are with us, and so's Amy. And Kate, but she doesn't count – she thinks it's all about Enid Blyton and Mallory Towers!"

"So what next?"

"Lesson 4. The bell's gone."

"So what is it?"

"English."

Ben's voice was flat: "Without Mr Luxmore."

"Yes. Without Mr L. Ben, why don't you come and see Mrs L? She'd like to see you."

"No, El. I'll leave that to you and Poppy and Henry and the others."

103

"All right. But we mustn't forget her, or him. There's still something wrong somewhere about the whole business."

"What do you mean?"

"I don't know. It's just the timing I suppose. Just when Mr L. was about to help us with Letty and all that. And it would be Danny who was out on the road at that time, so early. One car, one tractor, and they hit."

"Could've just been an accident."

"Could've. Could've been on purpose too."

"Do you really think so, El?"

"I don't know, Ben, I just don't know. But I'm going to find out. And, Ben?"

"Yes, El."

"Much though I adore you, my name is Eleni, not El."

"Yeah, I'm sorry. Eleni it is then. Elegant Eleni," he added provocatively.

"That's me," she said with a flirtatious wave of her hair. "That's me." And Eleni she would always be from then on.

12

It being the middle of June the Kow Klub was in session.

Their settlement on the steep, wooded slopes of the spinney looked more like a primitive village than a camp. It was out of sight of the prying eyes of the school, almost half a mile round a curve in the river bed. It was a place no prowling duty master saw even if they happened to walk round the grounds – in summer the thick foliage of the ancient trees at the bottom of the slope hid the encampment, which was a hundred metres up the slope, from casual passers-by. There were several different constructions.

The two berth variety were tent-like and made from rows of straight branches sloped like tepees and covered with moss and fern; at the top where the spinney bordered on a field of wheat there were two rooms with flat floors, dug into the bank. In the camp thick branches nailed to trees provided support for roofs made from discarded sheets of corrugated plastic. These rooms, each big enough to shelter about six children sitting on boxes, held the Kow Klub supplies. They had a waterproof tuck box, cleverly unmarked to fool intruders; there was a white plastic container used to collect rain water; there was even a loo roll on a stick which got wet when it rained, but dried out quickly in wind or sunshine. There was also a box with newspaper and dried twigs for their illegal camp fires.

Several platforms had been dug out of the slope to provide flat areas for those rare times when bedding down under the stars with sleeping-bags was allowed at weekends. These moments were a mixed blessing for the Kow Klub as a member of staff had to be present to fulfil the strict Health and Safety regulations.

The Kow Klub consisted mainly of the more eccentric members of the community - the team games drop-outs, children who liked hill-walking, astronomy, poetry and one or two who stayed for Holy Communion after they had already endured the compulsory service on Sunday mornings, down in the local church. Their interests and views were diverse and unusual, but they shared a common antipathy towards the school's authority, especially when it came to rugby which they detested.

Their founder member was Twig who had disgraced himself in his one and only rugby match when he was ten and playing for the Under 11C team. He had found himself with the ball and was totally at a loss as to what to do with it, so when one of the St.Peter's team rushed at him growling "Give it 'ere!" Twig had smiled politely and handed the offending article to someone who obviously wanted it more than he had. Brocky had never forgiven him, but luckily his disapproval took the form of completely ignoring Twig, which suited both of them perfectly.

Since then membership of the club had increased slowly, by invitation only, until there were eleven of them. Today's group consisted of Chloe, Kate, Poppy, Adeola, Henry and, of course, Twig himself. The three Ridicules were occasional guest members, sometimes needing refuge from lurking authority in the shape of Sweaty Vestey and Cupcake.

On this occasion only Leo had ventured down to the spinney. The camp was a natural breeding ground for protest and rebellion, but it was also a place for discussion, debate, adventure and toasted marshmallows. For once Leo was without his guitar and Chloe without a book; marshmallows could destroy such items with ease as toasting forks, hands and mouths became covered with sugary stickiness. It was after games on a Wednesday and it had been a fine, hot day. A log fire was glowing red hot as four toasting forks competed for flame.

Twig Beech, in his element out in the wild, was unusually talkative.

"I fink that Cupcake is a weasel," he said with calm conviction. The others laughed at this unprovoked attack on the Deputy Head.

"Don't be silly, Twig. How can a cupcake be a weasel?"

"Because Twig likes mixing metaphors," said Chloe, "don't you?"

"Not really," continued Twig. "I just want to slag him off a bit."

"Why?" asked Chloe.

"Because he sneaked to Matron that he fought I had a phone at school, and she looked in dorm and found it. Two weeks off tuck," he grumbled.

"Why didn't you mention it before?" asked Henry.

"Because I've been plannin' revenge," he said.

"On Matron or Cupcake?"

"Cupcake."

"What are you going to do?" asked Poppy incredulously.

But before he could reply a huge figure smashed into view yelling ferociously.

"Yes! You little rat! What ARE you going to do?" It was Vestey, red-faced, spitting and quite terrifying brandishing a heavy stick which, in his huge hands, swept dangerously near to the children. The children were frozen in terror, their toasting forks discarded, marshmallows melting in hissing flames. "Well?" he continued. "Well?"

"Sir, I..."

"I WHAT! Speak up, I can't hear you! You dirty little vermin." He glared round at the rest of the group. "And you lot, you nasty bunch. RATS, all of you. You are all part of this." As he stormed and shouted at them he lashed out with his foot and kicked earth and stones into the angry flames. He looked around for the first time at the Kow Klub's precious camp.

"So this is where you've been skulking, is it? I might have known. All the wasters and louts. Well never again. This place is finished." Poppy, overcome with terror, began to wail uncontrollably. Vestey smiled cruelly and turned on her. "Yes, you stupid cry-baby, cry your eyes out!" Again he lashed out with his foot, showering Poppy with dust and debris. But before he could say another word Adeola jumped to her feet and screamed:

"Leave her alone, you bully! I hate you! I hate you!" She was slightly down the slope from Vestey and although she was a big girl for her age she looked minuscule beside the towering figure of Vestey. He stared at her in mute surprise for several seconds, then he slowly raised his stick with which he could have easily killed her. Adeola, shaking with fright and sobbing with emotion, held her ground and spoke slowly but firmly, eyes wide with fear:

108

"You...can't...hit me! Teachers...can't...hit children." There was a tense silence while Vestey stared at the trembling Adeola. The remnants of the marshmallows continued to hiss and splutter under the embers and scattered earth. He breathed in and out, deeply. Then he spoke in a voice that was full of menace and hatred.

"Of course I won't hit you, you stupid little cow! You'd like that, wouldn't you! You'd be hurt, but you'd win. No, I'm not going to touch any of you." He stared round at the tense, broken circle of children. "But what I am going to do is this: I'm going to make your last few weeks here Hell. I heard you threaten the Deputy Headmaster, that's bad enough. On top of that you have been consuming illegal sweets - from one of your stupid parents, I suppose – and burning an illegal fire. You know what the rules are. And you have broken several." He paused to watch the effect of his words. No one had the temerity to speak now; they knew that Vestey had won. "Now." His voice grew even quieter as he sensed victory. "I want you all to get off this hillside, go back to school and wait outside the Headmaster's study. And no telephoning Mummy," he added, with searing sarcasm. "Now, go!"

The defeated and dusty group got to their feet. Leo put a comforting arm round Poppy who was still crying. He knew he was breaking the "no touching" rule, but Vestey had shot his bolt and said nothing. They moved disconsolately down the slope until they were hidden by the trees. Behind them they could hear the sound of Vestey smashing wood, destroying their years of work. They knew he wouldn't stop until it was all gone, and every last stick was broken.

"Twig," said Henry gently, "don't worry, we can build it up again. But Twig, beyond tears, ignored him and strode on staring straight ahead. As the silent group made their way along the track back to school none of them looked at the Acorns' little enclosure with its log benches and nature table. None of them saw the Acorns' swing either with Sarah sitting on it and Joe standing behind her holding the swing still. Dog waited until the group had passed before swinging his legs off the table, jumping to the ground and giving the thumbs up signal to the other two.

"Got 'em!" he said. "Stuffed good and proper. Too big for their damned boots"

13

The school was in turmoil.

The rebellious miscreants were standing in a straight and grim-faced line outside the Headmaster's office. A bored and restless duty master, Brocky, was standing guard to make sure no one communicated with them. Taking things to his usual extreme extent he had banned anyone from even coming in visual range: the corridor was empty.

But outside, in the yard, there was wild activity as news spread rapidly and wide-eyed children eager for news collided with others intent on playing their usual ball games. The staffroom was unusually full for the time of day and raised voices could be heard exchanging heated comments. Argument in the staffroom always elicited a lively response from the children, and when Miss Garforth unwisely emerged into the yard she was immediately surrounded by a horde of children yelling questions.

"Miss G, Miss G! What's happened to the Kow Klub?"

"What did they do?"

"Who caught them?"

A flustered Miss G fought them off as best she could.

"Look, I just don't know! Go away and play! It's nothing to do with you."

"But Miss...!

"No! I've nothing to say. Now let me through." Her plea fell on deaf ears as more and more gathered to hear anything that she might divulge. But before the flustered Miss G could be completely swamped an angry Mr Kupp shot out of the Staffroom and yelled:

"You have five seconds to disperse. Five...four...three..." They all knew what the penalty for disobeying Cupcake was, and Miss G was soon left by herself with only the Deputy Head for company.

"Thank you, Colin, that wasn't pleasant," she muttered, embarrassed.

"My pleasure, Sally," Mr Kupp said with an oily smile. "But perhaps you should go home now. I am sure all will be resolved in the morning."

"I hope so. Mike Vestey was in an awful mood though."

"Sally..."Mr Kupp hesitated. "Sally, I think you should just go home." Sally, who was obviously upset by proceedings both in and out of the staffroom, sighed, turned and headed quickly for the car park.

Mr Kupp glared round the yard, grabbed the hand-bell from inside the staffroom door and rang it vigorously.

"First bed bell. Go now." It was ten minutes early but no one was arguing. And anyway, sensitive ears had picked up the fact that Vestey was in a bad mood. That in itself was something to discuss in the relative privacy of the dorm. The seniors, faced with a sneering Cupcake, dispersed to their classrooms or to the Senior Common room.

In the Staffroom discussion and been replaced by disagreement, disagreement by confrontation. Vestey was fuming:

"I don't care what you say. They broke the rules and were insolent. They are demob happy." But Miss Peruzzi was standing up for the children.

"Oh, for goodness sake, Mike! They're only children having some innocent fun. Marshmallows over a fire! I wouldn't mind some myself!"

"That's not the point. They were being disrespectful to a member of staff." Mr Cooper emerged from behind his Telegraph and spoke tiredly:

"If you hadn't been eavesdropping you would never have heard them. Children say things like that. Can't you let it go?"

"And you destroyed their camp. That was wicked," continued Miss Peruzzi. "They have spent years making that."

"Yes," Mr Kretchner interjected. "With stolen nails, planks, loo rolls and God knows what else."

"Oh, for Heaven's sake!" You've no proof they've stole anything."

"Circumstantial evidence, my dear lady, circumstantial evidence. Where else could they have got it from but the school grounds?"

Miss Peruzzi, in a minority of one, was beginning to waver.

"They pay the fees...or their parents do. What harm have they done? And please do not call me 'my dear lady'. And, Tina, stop smirking in that ridiculous way!"

Tina Wilde was indeed smirking. She knew the power that Mike Vestey had in the staffroom hierarchy and liked watching him bullying weaker members of the staff into submission.

"Sorry, Jenny dear. I do like a bit of comedy, that's all. Brightens up an otherwise dull day."

113

"Oh, you ridiculous girl," retorted Miss Peruzzi. "In thrall to your Lord and Master again, I see." Tina rose to the bait:

"What exactly do you mean by that?"

"You know perfectly well. Where Mike leads, little Tina follows after."

"You bitch! How dare you!" Tina shouted, jumping up.

Jenny, observing the effect her remark had had ignored the insult and merely raised her eyebrows and smiled.

"If the cap fits..."

"You bitch, you absolute bitch!"

"Now, ladies," sighed Mr Cooper. But it was too late. Tina Wilde stormed out of the room taking the first door, which led to her room above the Staffroom. Through the other door lay the enemy, little people, a constant source of interference in her life.

Vestey, having enjoyed watching the cat fight, gathered his books and, with a self-satisfied "I think that's the end of that" also left. Those still in the room, including the humourless Mrs Woznak, Head of Music, who had watched the whole scene with no change of expression whatsoever, returned to their little islands in the voluptuous confines of the large and tatty armchairs, and silence once again descended. Jenny Peruzzi, tight-lipped and head held high, walked slowly to the door. A tear was in her eye, but she was not going to let anyone know. They were only children, she thought, only children.

"Well. I have to say, I am most displeased." The Headmaster's voice sounded more tired and bored than angry, but that could change if any of the miscreants said the wrong thing. And 'the wrong thing'

114

in Watsham' eyes was almost anything that was not an abject apology. Excuses and complaints were a no-go area. The Kow Klub prisoners awaited their fate with resignation. Vestey's anger and cruelty had knocked them all sideways.

"I had hoped at the beginning of this term..."

Here we go they all thought – pompous lecture that will last about ten minutes and that we have heard one hundred times before.

"...and I intend to punish you by wasting your time as you have wasted mine."

End of lecture. Imposition of punishment.

"You will each spend the whole of tomorrow copying out the Stonegate Code of Conduct two hundred times. And you will do it perfectly, because I shall check it and mistakes will lead to rewrites. I am particularly disappointed by you, Poppy, I had thought better of you. Your parents will be very upset by your behaviour."

"Yes, Sir," said Poppy meekly without looking up.

"Well, you all know what you have to do?"

"Yes, Sir," they all replied monotonously.

"Now go," stated Watsham as he turned to his desk.

They had almost reached the door when Leo turned.

"But, Sir...?

"Yes, Leo, what is it?"

"Tomorrow's the Leavers' London trip."

"Precisely," said Watsham as he looked up with a supercilious smile on his wrinkled face. Leo met his gaze for several seconds before turning and leaving.

The yard was quiet. It was time for dorm and the friends said a quick goodnight before going their separate ways. When the girls arrived in their dorms their sullen mood was greeted by an equally dismal mood already firmly occupying the dorm.

Kirsty looked up from her book: "What did you get?" she said with little enthusiasm or interest.

"Two hundred bloody 'Codes', during the London trip" said Kate, subdued for the first time anyone could remember. She was dyslexic and would take twice as long to do them as the others would.

"Oh," Kirsty said and returned to her book.

"Well, hello," Chloe said sarcastically. "Is there anyone in?"

Letty looked up and sighed: "Sorry, you lot," she said. We know you've had a bad time, but so have we."

"Why? What's happened?"

"It's Mrs Luxmore," Letty continued. "She won't see us any more."

"What do you mean?" asked Poppy who loved her meetings with Mrs Luxmore, and her occasional visits to the hospital to see Mr L.

"What I say," continued Letty. "She won't see us. We tried to go after games – you know, our usual time – but she just opened the door a crack and said it 'wasn't convenient'. Said she was tired."

"We accepted that," added Kirsty, "but as we went back up the path she said something else."

"Well, what?" asked Kate.

"Said she didn't think it was 'appropriate' any longer for us to see her, or Mr L."

"Couldn't believe it," said Letty, visibly upset.

"So," said Kirsty in as matter-of-fact a voice as she could muster. "Looks like we've lost our only friend, our only real friend on the staff. And we've lost Mr L too."

"But why?" Kate persisted.

"Don't know," said Kirsty. "Could be fear of the Headmaster, or Vestey. Could be depression, sort of giving up."

"Or maybe she's just fed up with us. Maybe she's just had enough...of us."

Eleni said nothing. She was listening. Vestey had destroyed the Kow Klub. The group of seven had had the wind knocked out of them. Mrs Luxmore had deserted them. So, she thought, nothing to lose.

Later that night Eleni slipped silently out of bed, put on her dressing-gown and trainers and left the dorm. The long, carpeted corridor had a ghostly glow from the dim safety lights, and pale starlight added to the sense of mystery and silence. Fully practised in escaping from dorm she moved quickly past the loose creaky floorboards, fled downstairs and was soon out of the door under the warn night sky. The constellation of Orion shone brightly above her, and in her loneliness felt a strange kinship with the distant stars. As she moved, so did the constellation, as if it was watching over her. She knew it was an optical illusion, but still felt that the solid reality of the stars, however distant, was a comfort beside the evil that assaulted her senses whenever she thought about the institution that was Stonegate Hall. There were bad people, doing bad things and she had resolved to sort it no matter what the cost.

She had no particular aim on this night, but ten minutes of wandering found her outside the Luxmores' house. She opened the garden gate carefully. The normally colourful flowers were a uniform blue-grey, framed by deep shadows behind, but she was not frightened. If anything she felt calm, liberated from the cares that wracked her every waking moment. Was Mrs Luxmore awake? She drifted silently round the house looking for tell-tale lights, but the house was in darkness. Mrs L must be asleep. Or, more likely, awake, eyes wide staring at the ceiling. Why had she rejected the children? It was not like her. Something was wrong, and she, Eleni, had to find out what it was. But now was not the time. With newly strengthened resolve and with the stars still following her she went back down the hill, slipped back into the house and was in her dorm and had fallen into a deep, dreamless sleep within two minutes of entering the building.

14

The Stonegate Hall Code of Conduct

1. Show respect for all others, especially towards those in authority.

2. Always endeavour to give of your best in everything you are asked to do both in work and play.

3. Do not abuse, damage or deface school or anyone else's property.

4. Always thank people for what they do for you: in class, at meal times, on the games field and elsewhere.

5. Do not use foul or abusive language at any time.

6. Be neat, tidy and polite at all times.

7. Be kind and thoughtful.

Leo had reached one hundred and twenty six before lunch. He was relaxed about it all. So he'd missed the London trip. Unavoidable. That was life. London would still be there after he'd left Stonegate. And it was good being with his friends like this, even though they were on silence. It was still possible to exchange glances, especially with Poppy.

He'd had time to think about what he was writing too in the first afternoon session. It all seemed a bit pompous and dictatorial. And surely it was designed for the welfare of the teachers rather than the pupils. It all seemed to be there to help keep the bricks and mortar that was Stonegate Hall together, rather than to keep the souls of the wicked children pure. Oh, yes, except for the last one, slipped in as an afterthought 'Be kind and thoughtful'. Yeah, not a bad one that, Leo thought. But why was it last? And wasn't Stonegate a Christian foundation? Didn't 'love one another' just about cover the lot (especially when it came to Poppy, he thought, grinning to himself)? Leo realized, even with his limited experience of life that the stricter the moral code that was imposed the more immoral the institution seemed to be. Who had invented this code, he wondered? Probably Vestey, Kupp and Watsham, with the icing of the seventh rule added by Miss Peruzzi and granted to her as a sop by the others to stop her ranting on about "What's right for the *children*".

The sun was streaming in the window of the dark-panelled prep. room where they had been incarcerated. Supervision was minimal, but there was nothing to be gained on this occasion by annoying the staff. The day slipped sleepily by. Time slowed to a hesitant shuffle. Even the sharp scratching of the pens had changed to a more even, lazier dragging of inky nibs across tired paper.

The sun had begun to slide down the sky when a tired Mr Attingham came to dismiss them. They were all in such a heat induced stupor by this time that they did not react immediately. But wearily in ones and twos they eventually started to clear their tables and, as they passed the teacher's desk and dumped their papers, they drifted off to what was left of the day.

Twig wanted to be by himself.

He had been badly hurt by the destruction of the Kow Klub. His feet took him to one of his favourite places, the tractor sheds – strictly off limits, but usually deserted on a Sunday. The heat bounced off the concrete outside the huts and, yes, the big doors were all shut. But one small gate at the side was open. Good, thought Twig. Exploration! He poked his head round the corner and sniffed the glorious mixed scent of machine oil and cut grass. It drew him in. He tiptoed into the centre. The two tractors stood, larger than life in this confined space and Twig stood transfixed drinking in the atmosphere. But with a shock that froze the blood in his veins he saw, not ten feet from him but with his back turned, a figure hunched over a trestle table oblivious of Twig. He was cutting something, and there were three or four small brick-like parcels beside him wrapped in silver foil. It was Danny. Twig let out an involuntary squeal of terror and Danny whirled round, knife in hand.

"Who the f...?" He looked with anger and disgust at the small, round trespasser.

"You come in 'ere you little bastard?" Twig couldn't move. Instead, Danny moved towards him, speaking menacingly as he approached. "What've you seen? 'ow long 'ave you been standing there, spying? Tell me!"

"I wasn't...I didn't...see nuffing..." Twig stuttered.

"I don't believe you, you lying little kid. You are all a bunch of lying little spoilt brats!" He was now inches from Twig's face. Twig was whimpering quietly.

"No...really...I..."

"Just shut it will yer. I've got to think about this I 'ave. So you saw nuffing did yer!"

"N...n...no!"

Danny tried another tack:

121

"What were you doin' in my shed?"

"Just came to see the tractors," Twig gasped desperately.

"Wha'for! Come on, tell me. You've no right to come in 'ere."

Twig was at a loss to know what to say. He was terrified and had no idea why Danny was being so aggressive. He could smell Danny's sweaty stench above the usual smells of engine oil and grass. He could still see the blade in his hand, rusty but sharp.

"Well," Danny persisted. "Wha'for!"

"I...I...jus' like tractors," he whimpered. "I always have done. We got one on our farm. Two actually. I...want to learn to drive them...I..."

"I don't want no friggin' family history. I just want the truth you little squit."

"It is the truth, I swear it." Twig looked up at Danny imploringly, begging him with his eyes to believe him.

"Well you listen to this, Twig Beech. You listen. If I hear that you 'ave said A WORD about what you've seen 'ere. I will mark your fat little face with this rusty knife. I will find you and I will do it. Got it 'ave yer?"

Twig nodded vigorously.

"Now get out, and never come back in 'ere."

Twig left. He was terrified. His mind was full of two things – the dangerous looking knife, and the foil parcels. Why had Danny got so angry over them? Just a few crumby parcels? Anyway, whatever they were Twig wouldn't say a word to anyone, ever.

He hid beside the squash courts and watched as, five minutes later, Danny got into his small hatchback and raced off noisily down towards the village and beyond.

122

Meanwhile the rest of Year 8, some twenty-six boys and girls, had been having a happy day in London.

They had Miss Peruzzi in charge, with Mr Cooper in tow, and Matron Julie, who was taciturn but harmless, in case of any sickness. They had come up from Dorset by an early train and were in Trafalgar Square by ten o'clock. They had a busy programme, but all the items were within a short distance of each other, and ice-cream kiosks abounded to keep the energy levels up. Not that the exuberant Miss Peruzzi needed any sugar top-ups. She was entirely powered by caffeine, and kept up a running commentary of enthusiasm and inspiration throughout the day.

First was a lightning visit to the National Portrait Gallery where Mr Cooper's brief lecture on the Elizabethans was interrupted by Miss's pigeon-like cooing over the colours of Good Queen Bess's dresses. Then the Impressionist wing in the National Gallery, where the children chose the rather lurid "Execution of Lady Jane Grey" as their favourite. Next a brief respite with a free piano concert in St.Martin-in-the-Fields, where several children drifted off to sleep despite the hard wooden pews. Then lunch in St.James' Park where pigeons and squirrels shared the picnics. Lunch over, down into Churchill's Cabinet War Rooms, left almost untouched since the Second World War, and into the interactive museum where Ben pressed the Hiroshima nuclear bomb button three times causing the loudspeakers to rattle on their hinges, despite Eleni threatening to never speak to him again. Another ice-cream, a walk through Horse-Guards Parade, across Trafalgar Square (photographs of children sitting on Landseer's lions), down into the underground, to Waterloo, and the long train journey back to

Dorchester where Toby Watt, diminutive rugby scrum-half, was almost left on the train but was found asleep under a seat just before the whistle blew.

And with morale and mood temporarily restored after a fantastic day, twenty-six boys and girls arrived back at Stonegate, sleepy, but stuffed with memories. And on this occasion they all obeyed the fourth clause of the Stonegate Hall Code of Conduct by thanking the staff profusely for a wonderful day before disappearing up to dorm, pockets still stuffed with sweets, at ten-thirty p.m., almost exactly seventeen hours after having emerged from them.

Eleni woke up early next morning, and all memories of London disappeared in a puff of dreams as she remembered what she had to do that morning. She quailed at the thought of disturbing Mrs Luxmore but knew she had to. The quiet but steadfast Poppy would accompany her, but stay back at the crucial moment. One was enough, two probably too many.

Break saw the two friends nervously approach the Luxmores' garden gate, and tentatively push it open. Poppy stopped just inside the gate, patted Eleni and whispered "Good luck!" before pressing herself gently behind the azalea bush. She watched as Eleni moved forward slowly towards the front door. She knocked gently and waited. Nothing. She was about to knock again when Poppy saw the familiar shape of Mrs Luxmore moving slowly behind the corrugated glass. The door opened just a few inches. Eleni moved forward and spoke. In her position by the gate Poppy could not hear anything. A few quiet exchanges. Then suddenly Poppy could hear, and things began moving quickly:

"But you must listen!" said Eleni loudly.

"No! No! I don't want any more of this!" Mrs Luxmore sounded upset but almost spat the words out.

"Please!" Eleni begged.

"No! It must stop!" Poppy had heard enough. This was not what was meant to happen. Without knowing what she was doing she rushed forward and grabbed Eleni firmly by the arm.

"Eleni! Stop. Come with me now!" Poppy glimpsed Mrs Luxmore through a diminishing crack in the door. Eleni was wild eyed and beginning to panic.

"But Poppy I..."

"Not now. Just go. Go!" Eleni hesitated, then burst into tears and ran from the garden. But Poppy, breathing heavily, stayed. The door was now closed, Mrs Luxmore gone. Without thinking Poppy walked forward and knocked on the door, as firmly as she dared. There was an immediate response from the shadows just inside.

"Go away. I've told you. I've had enough." Poppy heard the unmistakable sound of sobbing through the glass panels. She thought for a second before speaking.

"Mrs Luxmore. It's me, Poppy, your friend. You don't have to let me in but please listen. I don't know what has happened. I don't know why you won't speak to us. But I do know that we need your help, desperately... Whatever has happened, I know that neither you nor Mr L has done anything wrong. You are our last hope. Please talk to me...it's just me, Poppy... I'm not going to go away. Please."

There was still an intermittent sound of sobbing from behind the door. But after a minute or so, it grew quieter, and then there was silence. Poppy waited. Then the tired, corrugated shadow appeared again, the

125

door handle turned and a face of infinite sadness appeared. Poppy was taken aback.

"I...I'm sorry, Mrs L...I'll go now. I'm sorry." She turned to go.

"Poppy!" A voice to match the face, full of weariness and misery. Poppy turned back.

"Poppy. Come here, dear. Come in. It might as well be you who hears first." Poppy stared in disbelief.

"No, Mrs L. he can't have. He was doing so well..."

"No, no, Poppy. Andrew is alright. It's not that. Come in, dear. I've something to tell you. But you must be brave. You may not like what I have to say." The door opened, and Poppy went in.

15

Eleni, red-eyed and distraught, lay full length on the library sofa. Sitting in three chairs facing her were Ben, Amy and Alec. Eleni was almost hysterical, breathing deeply, eyes shut, beyond tears.

"It's over. It's over, I tell you... There's nothing left to do... They've won."

"Who's won, Eleni? What do you mean?" Ben was mystified.

"The whole rotten lot. Vestey, Watsham, Wilde. All their drugs and sex and abuse. We can't stop them. They've got away with it. I just want to leave, get out of this Hell-hole. I want to die."

"No, you bloody don't!" said Ben vehemently. "Don't say that stuff! Just shut it!"

"Ben, she doesn't need that," said Amy. "Just let it go." Ben lapsed into an angry silence. Eleni's breathing slowly calmed. The four friends sat in silence as the daylight faded. Eventually they were in deep shadow, the bright library colours faded and greyness filled the room. Action had failed and stillness was the obvious alternative. At least they were together. Togetherness banished despair, temporarily. At last Eleni slept, and the others sat, lost in their thoughts.

Minutes that could have been hours passed.

Then breaking the silence Ben turned in his chair as the huge oak door slowly opened. A figure slipped through the gap, unidentifiable in the gloom. A moment later the room was flooded with brightness as the lights were switched on.

"Poppy," said Ben. "What are you...?"

"They said you would be in here," Poppy said as the others stirred themselves, and Eleni dragged herself from sleep. Poppy stayed by the door leaning back against a bookcase. There was something strange about her. There was a distant look in her eyes, as if some vision had invaded her mind and held her.

"What's up, Poppy?" Ben said, puzzled. "You look as if you've seen a ghost."

"No," she said, breathless. "No. No ghost."

"Come on Poppy," said Amy encouragingly. "What is it?"

"Something has happened. Something big. Mrs Luxmore she..." Poppy stopped. As they watched her a faint smile appeared on her face and her eyes shone. "There's a DVD. It was in Mr L's briefcase. All this time it's been there. She only found it last week."

"What are you talking about?" said Alec. "What DVD?"

"It's something really nasty, she wouldn't say exactly what – wouldn't let me see it," said Poppy, "I s'pose it's porn and if it is I don't *want* to see it. She was frightened. She thought it must have been Mr L's, that's why she shut us out – she was so ashamed, she said, but it wasn't his. I worked it out and told her. Don't you see? That's what he found that night, the night he was hurt. He'd found it and was going to go to the police, but he was almost killed instead."

"Oh, my God!" Eleni exclaimed, fully awake now. "Oh, my God!"

"Well whose is it then?" said Alec angrily.

"I don't know. But it's got visible fingerprints, and a handwritten label. Mrs L has phoned the police.

128

She doesn't dare drive because of what happened to Mr L. It's out of our control. They're coming, now."

"Jesus!" exclaimed Ben. "Who did Mr L see in the holidays? Someone's going to get it! Kretchner, Kupp, Vestey, maybe even Watsham!"

"Ben," said the relatively calm Amy. "It could be anyone."

"Yes, it could be," said Ben. "But it's *not* any of us."

Suddenly there was another figure in the doorway. It was Mr Kupp, flustered and angry.

"You lot. You are late for dorm. Go! Now!"

As they went Ben stared straight at the Deputy Head who met his gaze; but it was the Deputy Head who dropped his eyes first.

The police arrived late, after lights-out. But much to Twig's disappointment there were no blue flashing lights, and definitely no ambulances or fire engines. One unobtrusive car slid quietly up to the Headmaster's house and three figures, two men and a woman got out. They weren't even wearing uniforms but you could tell what they were, something about their posture and the way they looked around with glaringly obvious subtlety. They knocked on the front door. It was opened by the mousy Mrs Watsham. They went inside and the door closed. The boys could see it all from the top floor of the dorm block. It was "a bit of an anti-climax" said Twig, but Ben cheered him up by saying, "You wait, Twig. You wait." Then they all went to bed.

16

The next day there was no sign of the police.

And, unbelievably to the children, especially Poppy, there was no sign that there was anything wrong. The Headmaster was in breakfast as normal; so was Mr Kupp, and Vestey. Far from looking angry or worried they were relaxed and, if anything, more cheerful and talkative than usual. But, thought the perceptive Leo, perhaps they were *too* cheerful. Were they putting it on, showing a common front in the face of an attempt to bring them down? Did they know that Mrs Luxmore had contacted the police? She had made no attempt to hide what she had done. But only the inner circle of the children knew what she had done and why, so the staff didn't know – yet.

What had the police done? Had they arrested anyone? It seemed that they hadn't. Oh, what was the use? Letty thought. You could be abused, assaulted, humiliated and when someone was caught, nothing happened. *She* had most cause to be upset. Eleni and Poppy had told her about the DVD when they had come down to dorm. She had allowed her hopes to rise and let her believe that *something* was about to happen, that justice was going to prevail. But now, in the cold light of day, she realized that nothing had changed. She would leave Stonegate in three weeks, and live with the knowledge that the Headmaster's abuse of her would go undetected and unpunished forever. It was a bitter truth to accept.

She walked sadly to her form and sat at her desk, looking at the lines of ages etched into the lid. Had previous occupants of her desk felt like her? Were their other girls who had suffered in silence? She would never know. The bell interrupted her thoughts and she rose reluctantly to start the day.

Assembly was painfully normal – a bible story was read, badly and without any conviction, by Mr Kupp. Mrs Woznek bashed through the simple chords of "Oh, God our help in ages past, our hope for years to come" without inspiration, and this was reflected by the mediocre singing of the school. Kupp then mumbled through a few randomly chosen prayers. A few routine announcements ended the charade.

Then, as they all emerged from the gloomy hall into the sunlight, the children noticed the first signs of change, alteration from the routine. Outside the front of the school was a line of flashy cars – a Jaguar, two BMWs, a Bentley and a bright red Ferrari, cars that could only belong to eminent members of the Governing body of Stonegate Hall. They had cleverly sneaked into the school during assembly and avoided staff, and in the process, parents of day children too. With a few exceptions the governors were all judges or accountants or successful business men of one sort or another. There were one or two influential parents on the governing body too, generally landowners and farmers from around the south-west. Whatever had or hadn't happened, if these people were involved then the whole parent body would soon know about it.

All morning the cars were there, with their owners concealed from prying eyes in some inner sanctum of the Headmaster's house. Gossip increased, but only in furtive whispers and quick, snatched conversations. The staffroom was unusually quiet with none of the normal banter and laughter. There was always some pupil to denigrate or laugh about, some "Yummy Mummy" for the male staff to letch over, some past cricket match to dissect ball by ball. But today these things were forgotten. Rumour followed rumour; some staff were unnaturally quiet.

There was even a small knot of day parents out in the car park, stubbornly refusing to go home until they were sure there were no juicy bits of gossip to spread like a turbulent wind round the county.

The clandestine meeting lasted until it was time for games, a time beyond which it was sacrilege for any meeting to run. But games on this day was a desultory affair – the staff had other things to think about. The children changed into full kit as usual and made their way to cricket or rounders pitches. There was tennis for some too, and a swim for the juniors. But the usual excited noises that usually accompanied games was lacking on this day. It was humid, and there was tension in the air felt by staff and children alike.

The sleepy afternoon dragged on. It was nearly the end of games. Cricketers started packing their bags, the small swimming pool ejected the last weary children and the girls disappeared into their house to get ready for tea, and the day children for home.

Then the fire bell went and shattered the calm.

Children and staff stopped, not quite believing that either there was a fire or that anyone would be stupid enough to have a practice at tea and going home time. But all, except the young ones who were siphoned off to the music schools by Miss Dalton and Miss Garforth, dutifully went to their seats in the Theatre and sat quietly, waiting. Even the ancillary and ground staff were there (following the fire regulations) until after a quiet word from Mr Kupp they rose in

132

unison and quickly left. The head groundsman, Derek, had a visible haze of new mown grass trailing him as he disappeared into the slanting afternoon sunlight. Then the room fell into a deep, anticipatory silence. Heads turned, eyebrows were raised questioningly, but no one spoke.

Footsteps could be heard approaching, hesitating, moving on again until the Headmaster walked onto the stage, grim faced, and took his usual place behind the ancient, polished trestle table. He did not sit down.

"Here we go," thought Ben. "Here we go."

Watsham cleared his throat. And still he did not speak. Then his first words drew immediate gasps from the tense audience.

"I am afraid I have something very unpleasant and distressing to say to you." He paused and let his hooded eyes sweep round the hall, stopping for just a fraction of a second as he spotted Letty. She froze in terror.

"The Police came to Stonegate last night." More gasps. "Someone had sent them a DVD the like of which I have never come across before. It was a DVD of such distressing content that even the police, hardened as they are to such things, were by their own admission shocked."

"Oh, no," thought Ben. "This can't be happening. It can't. Oh, God Almighty."

The Headmaster continued, coldly and, for once, with impressive authority:

"The police invited our co-operation in trying to discover the source of this DVD. At no time, may I say, were I or any other members of the Stonegate staff, suspects. But the DVD did indeed originate from the school grounds. That much is certain." Another tense, calculated pause.

"I am forced, therefore, to fall back on the unhappy conclusion that a pupil at this school is somehow involved in this terrible matter. I hope," he continued, magisterially, "that I am wrong in this supposition. But until the truth is known this possibility must hang like a sword of Damocles above the heads of each and every one of you." Here, he pointed around the hall.

There was an even longer pause. His facial expression changed visibly from one of imperiousness to one of sympathy and sadness. There was even, Ben could have sworn, a tear in his eye.

"Now I know that to the great majority of you this must come as a terrible shock. Most of you - dare I hope *all* of you - are good, honest citizens. You come from splendid, supportive families. Some of you are third, even fourth generation Stonegate. Boys and Girls, I have no issue with you; you are the innocent victims of this just as much as I am." Here, a deep sigh. "All I ask of you is your help in rooting out this...this abomination, this stain on our good name."

"So the last thing I must say to you is this. If any of you know anything at all – anything – you MUST come forward and tell a member of staff as soon as possible. We must deal with and extinguish this blemish on the honour of Stonegate and everyone therein.

"You will now be sent to tea, or to your homes."

Stunned silence as the Headmaster left the stage.

Stunned silence.

Stunned silence from everyone left in the Theatre.

And in the back row the heart of Letty Applegate was breaking in two.

Mr Kretchner was the first to leave the Theatre. Best speech I've ever heard him make, he thought, bloody brilliant. It had pace, gravitas, authority and an outstanding use of dramatic pause. Sad that every last word of it was the most ghastly piece of disingenuous play-acting. A series of blatant lies. But, thank God, he thought, thank God that he said what he said.

17

Hope and then despair; hope, despair; hope, despair; would it never end, thought Amy?

It was several days after the announcement, Sunday morning, and Amy and the others were still in a state of shock and walking in a silent crocodile down to the village church for the Sunday service. Everything they had fought for had come to nothing. All their plans, their resolve had proved to be as ephemeral as a plume of smoke from a firework. Except their firework had been extinguished before the first rush of sparks had appeared. A damp squib.

Their only success had been that Mrs Luxmore's secret had been kept. She had sent the DVD anonymously and only the few of them had known; and since the Headmaster's speech they had made a pact not even to talk about it themselves. "Careless Talk Costs Lives!" they had learnt in the Cabinet War Rooms, and they were not going to let Watsham or anyone else find out where it had come from. If they did maybe the unconscious Mr Luxmore would still get the blame. Only they knew that he was innocent. And how *did* they *know* he was innocent? Purely because in their childish, no, child *like* state, they trusted him and knew without a shadow of a doubt that he was innocent. But that meant that someone else was guilty. Someone who would now never be caught. Even Eleni had given up. Her secret night-time wanderings had ceased. The children were broken.

And they knew, too, that there were illegal substances around still. Alcohol abuse was common; staff rolling back up the hill drunk from The Three Sailors in the village was a common occurrence. The evidence of drug abuse was there – suspicious meetings and movements of staff late at night, more often than not involving Danny, who had no official business being on the school site after five o'clock.

Less suspicious were the wild parties that several members of staff and some parents indulged in on a regular basis in the more distant properties of the Stonegate site. And then there were the dilated eyes and grey faces of Wilde, Vestey and others the morning after. And there was that residual smell drifting down the corridors. But if the DVD incident could be turned back on the children, so could any accusation that there were drugs on site. Any suggestion that any of the children had even seen cannabis would lose them their places at their next school. Hopeless.

But they were temporarily out of school! This was always the best bit about Sunday Church – they got to see the world outside the grounds of Stonegate, and some levity returned to all of them as they played the traditional street dares right under the noses of the accompanying duty staff.

The best game was Free the Flower. Certain boys (chosen by lottery every Saturday) had to collect flowers from gardens as they passed, using craft knives to deliver a quick sure cut so that bush wobble was minimal. Different flowers were awarded different points according to the rarity or exoticism of those collected. The judges were the girls whom the boys chose to present the flowers to on their return from church. The all-comers champion remained Biffo Swatridge's uncle who, allegedly, had ripped out six bright yellow tulips from one garden in one go when he was only eleven. He was caught, and subsequently beaten, when Matron spotted the flowers in a vase in the lucky girl's dorm, and recognized them as being those missing from her own sister's garden. He had borne his punishment with dignity and honour, and then married the girl sixteen years later.

There was also Crocodile Creep. The idea was to move forward as many places as possible in the strictly controlled two-by-two crocodile without being seen by duty staff. The three accompanying staff were meant to be evenly spaced in order to catch miscreants of any sort, but usually there were one at the front and two at the back talking to each other. It was possible to eat sweets, assault a neighbour, make faces at the drivers of passing cars and do almost anything short of actually leaving the crocodile altogether. The most daring achievement had been by two tinies from Year 5 who had, in the Spring Term, crashed through a hedge, run fifty yards along the edge of a field, crashed back through the hedge and emerged brambled, bleeding but triumphant at the head of the queue, in front of the prefects. None of the three duty staff had noticed a thing.

Many other activities and mere happy chattering helped the twenty minutes that it took them to reach the church pass quickly and, usually, joyfully. But once inside the ancient portals of the church of St.Barnabas the games had to stop. Matron checked their neatness before they were allowed in – hair was brushed, ties straightened, debris removed from blazers and shirts. Then they were marched to their pews where behaviour was carefully monitored by several staff, positioned strategically round the church. The whole of Year 8 were gathered in the south aisle, in the full glare of the morning sun, but out of the direct line of view of the parents.

On this particular Sunday nothing special was on offer. The children had learnt to accept that half-an-hour, incarcerated in mediaeval gloom could be tolerated with equanimity. The small, rotund vicar presided but it was the Headmaster, fashionably – but secretly - atheist, who welcomed everyone, including the usual scattering of parents, to the service. Then a hymn was sung by the choir and congregation. The Lesson was read by Sarah whose embarrassed smile showed that she was well aware of eyes looking even if ears were not listening.

Matthew (she said), Chapter 10, Verses 16-19:

Behold, I will send you forth as sheep in the midst of wolves: be ye therefore wise as serpents, and harmless as doves.

But beware of men: for they will deliver you up to the councils, and they will scourge you in their synagogues;

And ye shall be brought before governors and kings for my sake, for a testimony against them and the Gentiles.

But when they deliver you up, take no thought how or what ye shall speak: for it shall be given you in that same hour what ye shall speak.

Fear them not therefore: for there is nothing covered, that shall not be revealed: and hid that shall not be known.

Sarah read quietly but with excellent diction, her clear voice ringing round the sunlit stones. And when finished she fled to her pew happy, but completely unaware of the message she had just imparted.

For once Ben, Eleni, Alec and several others listened intently. They could hardly believe what they were hearing. The words had a resonance for them that they had never before experienced in a lesson in church. The message was that they should be brave and fight on and keep trying to delve into the darker corners of Stonegate life. It would all be revealed the reading had said. The readings always seemed to be so dry before. Although they did not understand the context or the full meaning of the words, some of them would remember them in the days to come.

Another hymn.

Then prayers.

Despite the vicar's presence, the Headmaster insisted on saying the prayers. These he intoned with exactly the right amount of piety (despite being an atheist) because there were parents listening.

But the Headmaster's atheism was not of the aggressive, intolerant kind. It was more an apathetic atheism that glanced at the fundamental questions of life, the universe and everything that was meant to be important and then put them in his out tray for someone else to deal with, while he turned to the back page of the newspaper to examine the cricket results.

The vicar's sermons always followed the same pattern. Today's was no different.

"My text is..." he started. And then he smiled beatifically before launching into a series of unfinished sentences and non sequiturs so involved and convoluted that it was the work of a genius to write it. But no genius would understand it. And it was long.

Amy was bored and she was not the only one. She could not listen anymore. What is the point of being here, she thought? If there is any truth to all this religion why does it have to be dull or complicated? And then she turned to her left and looked across the nave, into the shadows of the north aisle. And, irreverently, she imagined Jesus sitting, nodding off just as she felt like doing. Then someone coughed aloud and she was shocked back to reality.

She turned to gaze at the great stained-glass window in front of her. It was a depiction of a young girl and an even younger boy standing in a field gazing with innocent rapture at various animals that shared the field with them. There were three small, green hills in the distance. Amy knew who the children were – the son and daughter of the vicar of the village as they had been in 1847 when they had died within weeks of each other from tuberculosis. Had the girl been cast in an ideal light? Had she really been pretty, with long, dark hair? Not like me, thought Amy, small and skinny with short, mousy hair. But really it was the girl's eyes that drew attention – they were placid, accepting, at peace with the world. Had she really been like that towards the end of her short life of suffering? Oh, well, she was *now* anyway, and for all time too. As she looked, the sun came out and shone through the window and the motionless dust, covering the children of Year 8 in a hundred bright colours and all but blotting out the rest of the church.

That is beautiful, thought Amy, as she herself was bathed in light, and all the worries of the previous day melted away.

18

Sunday afternoon saw the Ridicules in conference.

They were in the trunk room and were sitting on three trunks, forming three sides of a square. The ceiling of this unique room was only five feet off the ground so standing was hazardous especially for Alec. It was tucked away in the recesses of the Victorian boarding block, up a small flight of stairs opposite the boys' sanatorium. No one was ill at the moment so the chances of being disturbed were remote, especially if they spoke in reasonably hushed tones. Leo, for once, did not have his guitar or even his iPod. They felt like beached fish slowly rotting in the sun, not even having the dubious pleasure of the anticipation of being eaten. They had come to the end of a journey, and no one cared, for good or ill. Their parents were busy preparing for *their* summers into which their offspring would have to fit, for good or ill.

"Mum is doing three festivals in July and August, and dragging me along," said Ben.

"What's wrong with that? Sounds fun," said Alec, thinking of eight weeks of summer at home, isolated, bored.

"Nothing, in a way. I like the one in Derbyshire. It's just that it's *her* music. No chance to scan the festivals for my sort of stuff. Lots of old rock and new folk I think. And mud, of course – but dear Mummy actually takes a Persian carpet for a groundsheet inside the tent, and has two doormats. No wellies allowed."

"Still think you're lucky," said Alec. "Mum and Dad are doing lecture tours, in Oxford and Munich. I'll stay behind alone, virtually; but I'm sure my wretched cousins will come over. They're a bloody pain. Might try to get Amy over – she's only 12.7 miles away."

"You've counted?" asked Ben, smiling suggestively.

"Yes, I have," Alec replied Alec matter-of-factly. "Where are you going, Leo?"

"Cornwall. Roc. Whole of August."

"Sounds great," said Alec.

"Some of it will be. It *sounds* good, I know, but you haven't met the Roc brigade that we go with. It's all hard partying, hard drinking, hard sailing as if the world was going to end in September." Ben looked from Leo, to Alec and back again.

"Well, that's it, is it?"

"What?" asked Leo.

"Yeah, what?" repeated Alec.

"All we've got left to talk about is shitty holidays, is it? Everything else is forgotten, eh?" He looked bitterly at them, accusing.

"Hey, Ben..."

"Don't you fucking 'Ben' me!"

"I was just..."

"Well forget it!" Ben lashed out with his foot at the trunk Alec was sitting on and smashed a hole in it.

"Jesus, Ben!"

"What!" said Ben lashing out again and again, denting, smashing. "What! What! Bloody what! – You know what! We've given up. All that fine talk about sticking together and sorting things. What have we actually done!"

"We tried, Ben," said Leo defensively.

"We tried, Ben!" mimicked Ben bitterly. "Do you know how pathetic you sound!"

Leo, cowed and suddenly a little ashamed, mumbled, "O.K., O.K. I know."

Ben looked at his friends once more, but they did not meet his gaze. "We call ourselves 'the Ridicules'. What for?" No reply. "It was meant to be because we made some of the wretched people here look ridiculous. We were meant to be fighting back against the bullies and the – what did Atlanta call them? – the tin gods and tyrants. And what have we done in fact? Eh? Nothing. We've been humiliated; everyone is laughing at us. We *are* the Ridicules, because we *are* ridiculous, pointless, an irrelevance." He spat out his final words with real venom: "*We are ridiculous!*" Crouching, he left the hot, dusty space and crashed down the stairs leaving a hot, tense silence in his wake.

Down in the girls' house Letty was alone in dorm. She was quietly packing a small rucksack. A waterproof, a wash bag with added make-up; an apple, two Mars Bars, cheese and onion crisps, a bottle of Fanta. Her purse with money. Her iPhone. A book. She took a small lock and chain from inside her bedside cabinet and slipped it into a side pocket of the rucksack. Then she changed out of her uniform and put on jeans, trainers, her favourite dark blue top with loose sleeves. She went out of the house to one of three garages reserved for the Headmaster. No need to open the door too wide. The bicycles in there were never used as far as she could tell. But they appeared to be in

144

working order. She chose a medium sized one with a dark blue frame. She checked the tyres – fine. Anyone around? No. She emerged from the garage, and gently closed the door behind her with one hand, holding the bicycle with the other.

"Time to go," she said to herself and she cycled off into the balmy evening air.

Although a few people wondered during tea where Letty was, they all knew that she often went off by herself and was happy in her own company. So no one was concerned about her until long after tea. By which time Letty was several miles away, cycling steadily. She was singing. Occasionally she actually laughed aloud. It would be dark before she reached the station, but she didn't mind. There was a clear sky, and a bright half moon was already visible rising in the east. The darkness would make her less conspicuous, but she would be able to see car lights approaching from some distance. She could stop and press herself against the hedgerow.

By the time the girls' house staff knew that Letty had run away it was half past six. There had been little helpful information from her friends. They wouldn't have said anything if they had known, but Letty had not told anyone what she was doing so they truly didn't know where she was.

"You are obfuscating!" their housemistress, Miss Dalton, claimed. "I want direct answers!"

"We will," said co-operative Head Girl, Kirsty, "but please could you tell us what 'obfuscating' means?"

Temporarily non-plussed Miss Dalton resorted to anger:

"Direct answers, I said! Where is Letty?"

"Direct answer: I don't know."

A search of the school grounds was instigated by available staff and interested pupils. When her uniform was discovered though, and it was noticed that her cabinet was almost empty, the alarm was raised and pursuit began. Mrs Watsham was sent in the school car, a powerful Renault, off towards the station. Although timid in company, Mrs Watsham was a demon driver and was sure she would be able to catch Letty before she got far. Walking or bicycling, she could not outpace the Renault. It was nine miles to British Rail, Dorchester, hills included; the car would get there way before that naughty, naughty girl, Laetitia Applegate did.

And Mrs Watsham did indeed arrive at Dorchester South railway station before Letty – at ten past seven to be precise. She paced up and down the platform in a considerable state of nerves convinced that Letty could not have reached there already. And she was right.

At ten past seven Letty was making slow but steady progress and was approximately three miles from Maiden Newton. It had been a longer route than going to Dorchester, but it was much prettier. By eight o'clock she had arrived, padlocked the bicycle and bought a ticket for Paddington (via Castle Cary). She went to the washroom where she quickly and quite expertly for a thirteen year old applied lipstick and eye shadow. She smiled at herself in the mirror, embarrassed at this sixteen year old that smiled back. Now, compose yourself: out onto the platform; just a scattering of people. Good.

She would catch the 20:34 and be in London at 23:19. She could walk home from there.

When she arrived empty-handed back at school Mrs Watsham was not happy, and, for once, bested her husband.

"Don't say any more!" she yelled at him. "She was not there, nor was she on the road."

"Well where the hell is the little cow then!" he complained.

"Obviously somewhere else."

"That is not helpful Camilla."

"It was not meant to be. I am tired."

"Damn! I'll have to phone her parents. That woman will keep me talking for hours."

"Yes, I'm afraid she will."

"What shall I say?" She gave him a hard stare.

"Tell him that their daughter has run away from school don't you think?" More heavy irony.

"Damn! Damn! Damn!"

19

There were plenty of spaces so Letty was able to choose a window seat, facing forwards.

The two seats opposite were occupied by a middle-aged couple. They were neat, and respectably dressed; the man wore a tweed jacket and a tie, the woman a dark, mottled dress and a coloured glass necklace to match. He was reading the Daily Mail, she, a Philippa Gregory book. Occasionally they would talk – about the view, about his sore back, about some minor celebrity scandal exposed in his paper, but most of the time they were quiet. They had both got on at Maiden Newton, smiled at Letty but then ignored her, which suited her fine. They were harmless.

Others that Letty could see included a man in his twenties, unshaven, wearing jeans and focussed on his iPhone. He was texting and playing games continuously. She could also see a coloured lady with braided hair and a small, restless boy aged about three. It was late for him. And there was a girl with straight, shoulder length brown hair. Probably still in her teens, Letty thought. All harmless looking then. No one to cause trouble for her, the runaway.

It was still quite light outside with the sun setting cosily into hazy cloud in the west, behind her.

So what now? She thought. What was she doing there? She realized suddenly that she didn't really know. She had acted instinctively. She'd just taken too much and she had to get away. Yes, that was it. But what was her plan? She had planned the details of her flight meticulously, but now she had done it there was a real uncertainty as to what she was going to do, and why.

Start thinking.

The Headmaster had abused her. Saying it to herself sent a shiver of fear, no, of revulsion through her. She knew about sex; the boys, she suspected, thought about little else. But sex was something for her future, something to wonder about, something that would develop alongside relationships and the blossoming of love. It was not for now. But he, he had isolated her, looked at her, touched her – what was the word? – 'inappropriately'. And no one cared. Couldn't they see those hooded eyes, the lingering glances? They *must have*. But they were too frightened or too indifferent to her situation to do anything. Vestey, Wilde, Kretchner, Woznak: well, of course them. But Mr Cooper, Miss Dalton, Miss Peruzzi: them too? And that was it, of course, why she was on the train: would her own parents do the same? Would they do the British thing and pretend that none of it had happened? Well, she would see, in about three hours.

She shook herself back to the present and found herself staring out of the window at the darkening fields. No one there. A gentle pastoral scene flashing by, with sheep wandering, cows grazing, birds beginning to roost. Lonely houses, farms, villages. Isolated, indifferent to each other's fate. Who cared about her? Her friends at school – they did! But, she realized, the ones who cared were also the ones who couldn't do anything to help. The ones with the power were the ones who didn't care, the abusers, the bullies, the liars. It was hopeless.

149

"Tickets from Maiden Newton, please." A portly and grumpy looking ticket inspector was staring at her. Panic. Where's the ticket? Where *is* it? Ah, here, quick. Damn! Dropped it.

"Nah, don't move, darlin', I'll get it." And down Mr Grumpy inspector went, onto one knee, retrieved the ticket, signed it, handed it back. Smiled, and said:

"There you are, Miss, put it away safe some place now." Another smile. "Remember to change at Castle Cary, won't yer? Couldn't 'ave yer racing off up north now, could we?"

"No. Thank you." Automatic response. He hadn't been grumpy, it had just been his face. He was friendly, not flirty, just friendly. And there he was, talking and laughing his way up the carriage. Not just her then.

But back to the shadow.

Concentrate.

Was he a bad man, the Headmaster? The school was doing well, they won matches, scholarships; all the local rich and famous sent their children there, and others who couldn't afford the fees competed for bursaries. And most of the children were happy most of the time. She had made friends that she would have for the rest of her life. Letty sat back and let this simple analysis of the state of things at Stonegate sink in as she tried to dispel the nightmares by the application of simple logic. And then, without willing it, tears began to brim, not tears of everyday hurt or sadness, but tears from some inner core that wrenched themselves out of her and, despite the look of shock on the faces of the couple opposite, they flowed down her face and she buried her face in her hands.

"Are you all right, dear?" from the woman; the man, concerned, worried but silent. But all she could do was to shake her head, unable to speak. She fought the well of despair that was engulfing her, and after several minutes she sat back, dried her eyes and said:

"Thank you very much for your concern, but I am all right now. I'm fine." And it was all right. She had purged herself, and she had come to a conclusion:

The good things at school were incidental, a product of many years, even generations, of effort and care by a thousand different people, good people. But corruption had taken over, in what different forms she didn't know yet; she knew that the insidious effect of this rottenness was beginning to tear the school apart, and at its core was the Headmaster. The Headmaster had abused her. What damage had been done to her? For his own gratification he had attempted to destroy her innocence and make her grow up faster than she could possibly bear. But he had failed. She knew that he had failed. But he was still culpable and she was going make him regret what he had tried to do. *She* was going to make him pay, not the staff, not her parents. He had attempted to damage her: she was going to punish him for it.

And sitting on the train with the middle aged couple, the mother and her son, the two young people, the ticket inspector, with the world rushing by outside, she saw that she was just one of millions, all with their own battles to fight, most of whom, most but not all, were on the side of the angels.

She got out her iPhone and sent one simple text: 'Don't worry – I'm fine. I'm coming back home. B there soon. Letty XXX.' She knew what she would say to her parents when she arrived home. It wouldn't take long.

When she got to London her father was waiting for her at the station. Having heard from the Headmaster he had guessed what Letty had done, worked out the times and had waited expectantly for the train to arrive. In fact it was two minutes early.

"Hello, Daddy," said Letty calmly.

"Hello, Letty, darling," he said, sighing. "Come on, I'll take you home."

"Yes, all right, but I'd like to go back to school tomorrow."

Mr Applegate stopped and stared at his daughter.

"You *are* a strange one," he said. "I don't think I understand you at all."

"No, Daddy, I don't think you do."

It was only a five minute drive from Paddington to their house in Inverness Terrace in Bayswater. A successful London lawyer, Mr Applegate enjoyed the city life, but still missed his home county of Dorset. His wife Amanda was a committed city dweller having lived in London, west of Marble Arch, all her life. Her daughter's arrival home at this unscheduled time was upsetting, especially at this late hour.

"Darling, what *is* this all about? We've been worried sick since Mr Watsham telephoned."

Mr Applegate watched his daughter's response carefully as he removed his coat and hung it up.

"I'm sorry, Mummy," said Letty quietly. "There've been problems at school, you see."

"No, I don't see, Darling, that's just the point. I thought you were really happy there, lots of friends and everything – and your scholarship."

"Mummy," she dived in, "the Headmaster is not a nice man. Basically...he fancies young girls. He's a paedo, Mum."

Astonished silence from Mummy. Raised eyebrows from Daddy. Mummy quickly recovered:

"Nonsense, Darling. He plays golf with the Barlow-Horswells, and Aunt Chloe knew his parents in Zurich – for years, they were good friends. What utter nonsense!"

"Yes, I thought you'd say that, roughly."

"It's just too bad, darling. There's only two weeks until you leave, and there's Sports Day to consider. And the Leavers' Service. Everyone'll know. We're meant to be having a picnic on the field with the Parrishes, the Tanners – Mrs Tanner is giving away the prizes – and the whatsisnames..."

"...the Hyltons."

"Yes, dear, of course, the Hyltons. It's just too bad." Pause for breath and a sigh. "It's no use. I've decided. Daddy's taking you back in the morning."

"Shouldn't we talk to Letty first, Amanda?"

"It's all right, Daddy, we can talk later when I'm in bed. Mummy?"

"Yes, what is it?"

"Why don't you ever listen to me?"

Letty's mother looked at her, uncomprehending.

"What *do* you mean, darling? We talk all the time."

"No, Mummy, we don't. You talk and I listen. You ask me what I want to do, and then you tell me what you have planned. And that is what I always do."

Again, Mrs Applegate clearly did not understand what her daughter was saying to her.

"Darling Letty, I think you are being a tiny bit ungrateful here. We have always put you first. Always. We have given you everything: holidays, friends, the best possible education..."

"Yes, Mummy, I know."

"Well, what *are* you talking about, darling?"

"Amanda, what Letty is trying to say, I think..." Mr Applegate started.

"Well don't think. No, don't think." With a wave of her arm Letty's mother turned her back on her family and busied herself rearranging several invitations of various sorts that were aligned on the shelf above the Aga.

Letty sighed and decided to speak to her mother's back.

"Mummy. I know what you have done. But don't you see? You seem to have everything planned, my whole life! You've even told me I'm going to Cambridge. I'm only thirteen." Silence, more nervous rearranging and shuffling of invitations.

"Mummy. Can you hear me."

Her mother turned wearily, to face her tiresome daughter."

"Well, darling you can't possibly go to Oxford. Your grandfather would turn in his grave. He was a Caius College man through and through." Mr Applegate groaned and prepared to enter the fray once again.

"Now look, dear..." It was Letty who interrupted this time.

"No, Daddy, it's all right. I will go back. I've decided."

"But, Letty..." her father began.

"No, Daddy, it's fine. I'll go back. I'm sorry for the trouble I've caused. I want to go to bed now. I'm tired. You can take me back tomorrow."

Twenty-five minutes later Letty was in her bed, in her room, with a mug of hot milk beside her. She had had a long day and she was very tired. She had had a quiet talk with her father, while her mother's voice could be heard talking on the phone in the kitchen using her social skills to wind up a stammering Headmaster back at Stonegate. But Letty was happy. She felt a sense of contentment akin to triumph infuse her whole being as sleep approached. Never in her life had she rebelled before. Never had she left the confines of home, school or planned activity before. It seemed to her that her whole life had been governed by adult decision.

Now she had made two decisions by herself – to run away, and to return – her decisions. And during that time, her time, she had seen the world in a new light. There'd been the people in her carriage, there'd been the lights on in a thousand little houses as the train flashed by, where people were talking, eating, working, going to bed. There was a world out there of people who had to decide things every day, things that could change lives, their own and other people's. And they did it and moved on. It was time for her to move on. But there was something she had to do first.

20

The first thing Mr Applegate and Letty did when they arrived back at Stonegate was to unload the bicycle. They had returned via Maiden Newton and retrieved the stolen article ("I only borrowed it," Daddy). They came in the back drive and slipped it sheepishly back into the Headmaster's garage before anyone spotted them.

Mr Applegate had agreed to report to the duty master while Letty went off down to the girls' house to get changed. She would be back in her uniform by break time.

On her way back up to school she could hear the shouts and screams of happily rioting children long before she saw them. An Acorns crocodile met her half way.

"Hello, Letty," said a grinning, Alfie as he skipped past, almost falling as he fixed his adoring gaze on her.

"Hello, Alfie." Even at this age, she thought, even at this age! And then she coloured, suddenly embarrassed as she realized that she could happily have picked the sweet little infant out of the crocodile and given him a squeeze.

The first person she met in the yard was Henry who was playing catch with a tennis ball against a wall.

"Hi, Letty," he said, matter-of-factly.
"Hi, Henry. How's things?"

"Fine." He threw the ball and the tall Letty stretched up and intercepted it. "We thought you'd be back. How far did you get?"

"Home. London," she stated simply.

"Wow! Brill!" he exclaimed. Then changing the subject in mid flight of the ball he said, "Alec and Amy are in with Watsham. They were caught in the library together and they weren't holding hands! Under a beanbag! I think Amy's pregnant!" Letty laughed.

"Wooooo!" she exclaimed. "Who caught them?"

"Mr Cooper. But Jeremy Stinton was peeping through the door and they think he snitched on them because he fancies Amy like craaazy but she hates him and I think Mr Cooper was laughing too really but he had to act as if they had broken the ten commandmants so he dragged them off to Watsham. *He* wasn't laughing." Up went the ball. Letty caught it, threw it up again. Catch, throw; catch throw. Catch. Henry turned to Letty.

"'s good about Mr L."

"What? What about Mr L?"

"You know, he's sort of woken up. Can't speak, but he can sort of look. Can move his fingers too." Letty stood, open mouthed.

"Henry, why didn't you *tell* me?"

"I *am* telling you, Letty."

"Great! That's wonderful," said Letty. "Where's everyone else?" Before answering, he threw the ball again. It hit a jagged piece of brick and ricocheted off into the yard. The friends chased it and within seconds a game of piggy-in-the-middle developed with about thirty yelling participants, with the shy Henry happy for once to be the centre of attention and Letty glowing with the good news about Mr Luxmore.

The end of term was only a month away, and everyone felt the approach of escape from the confines of school. Leo was sitting on a low wall playing his guitar surrounded by a small group of admirers. Behind him were a dozen or so small, square gardens which had been carefully tended throughout the summer term by small groups of children. Some had regimented rows of marigolds or pansies unsubtly stuffed into the soft earth. Others were more adventurous, with small landscapes including model bridges and miniature plastic-lined ponds. The best ones showed real artistry, with religiously nurtured plants of carefully graduated colour and size. These ones would win the garden prizes awarded by Mrs Luxmore on Sports Day.

Twig's garden would not win a prize: he had planted carrots and lettuces and he and others regularly harvested them. It was looking neglected. Twig was spending his time repairing the Kow Klub camp, refusing to accept that Vestey had destroyed his pride and joy and rendered it irreparable. He had begun by erecting a small shelter in the middle of the devastation from which he could sit and survey his shattered world. The shadow of Vestey haunted him whenever he stopped work. Why was he so angry? He just knew that he was terrified by his threatened violence, and the sanctuary of his beloved Kow Klub, whatever state it was in, was where he felt safest. Ten days would see him leave it forever with only its memory etched on his sad mind.

But most children were oblivious to his sadness as they played under the hot July sun. They rolled on the grass, flung Frisbees, played tennis, swam, hurdled, high-jumped, painted, read and gardened; they held surreptitious hands, whispered, wandered, loved and laughed. It was easy in this green paradise to forget the bad things in life and to push them away out of sight. And wasn't that one of the things that the children had already learnt from Mr Cooper's History lessons, that turning your back on monsters gives them time to feed and grow stronger?

Ben and Eleni were in their favourite place, with their backs to the rhododendrons which were dripping their blood red petals onto the grass. They gazed out over the fields with the blue, Dorset hills beyond. They thought they could see the sea, a thin, silver line on the horizon underneath mountainous cumulus clouds. They were momentarily content; they were with each other and out of sight of the school. Swallows skimmed the grass around them. Eleni broke the silence:

"Last chance really," she said simply. "I mean," she continued, "if we can't find anything by the weekend, it's all over."

Ben turned to look at her and smiled grimly.

"I'm going on another wander tonight," Eleni stated. "My last one. I know there's something. I think it's Kretchner."

"Bastard," Ben said.

"We know there are drugs. But where do they come from? I haven't seen needles so I don't think it's heroin. But it could be cocaine..."

"...and we know they've got cannabis," added Ben, warming to the subject.

159

"And the alcohol..."

"...pissed most nights now, Wilde, Vestey..."

"...the matrons, too, after lights-out." Their deliberations were interrupted by a thin, pale figure that suddenly appeared from the field side of the bulging shrubs.

"Hey, look. It's Letty. Hi, Letty. Good of you to come and visit," he added with irony.

"Hi, I've been looking for you two. I've just heard about Mr L."

"Brill," said Eleni, "but he's not safe yet. He can hardly move."

"But he's awake. But it's not that – I wanted to talk to you two about things."

"Why?" asked Ben. "Do you want to catch the plague?"

"What?" Letty was lost.

"The plague," said Ben with exaggerated horror. "We are the untouchables, the lepers!" He twisted his mouth and hands into grotesque parodies. Letty still looked puzzled.

"We are official outcasts," Ben continued. "Ignored by authority, deserted by those we called our friends. And talking of drugs and stuff..." Ben raised his eyebrows.

"Yes, Ben, what about them?"

"Well it's Smarties that does it for Stonegate children. A box of Smarties or Maltesers induces a trance-like state in any child. Even the huge frame of Biffo succumbs to the Smartie adiction." Letty understood at last.

"So, the revolution is over, is it?"

"Looks like it," said Ben.

"Not quite," said Eleni.

"Oh?"

"I've got a plan..."

"Well," said Ben, "it'll have to wait. Here come some Smartie addicts." Approaching suddenly from round the rhododendrons were Alec and Amy, closely followed by Leo and Atlanta.

There was a momentary, uneasy silence. It was broken by Atlanta.

"O.K., you guys, I know you've had a row, and I know what about. Leo told me. Oh, hi, Letty, you're back."

"What are you on about?" said Ben coldly.

"The Ridicules," Atlanta continued.

"What about them? They're officially disbanded."

"No, they're not. Just because you stamped out in a foul temper," said Leo angrily. Ben raised his eyebrows in surprise. He wasn't used to such instant hostility directed at him, especially from friends.

"Yes," agreed Alec. "You didn't give us a chance."

Amy joined in the assault:

"You were bloody nasty to Alec and Leo. You can be so arrogant sometimes." Ben looked at Eleni for some help.

"Ben," she said hesitantly. "Actually, they're right. You can."

"A conspiracy!" cried Ben, jumping up. "'Et tu, Brute' and all that! Brilliant!"

"Oh, shut up a minute. Stop being stupid!" This from mild, pale, demure Letty.

"Jesus Christ!" said Ben, astonished. "Letty hath a tongue!"

"I said shut up! Just fucking listen for once!" There was a stunned silence from the entire gathering. Letty simply did not use the 'F' word. It just wasn't in

161

her vocabulary. Until now. There were tears in her eyes, and she herself looked shocked by her outburst. But she shook her head and continued.

"You've been a shit for two terms. You've banged on and on about Vestey and drugs and Watsham and Wilde and all the rest of it. You've been a bloody pain. And now you want to give it all up, just because you, God Almighty Ben, says so? Well, go on, bugger off! We don't need you. Go to fucking Hell!" She was shuddering with emotion. A dam wall had burst after years of repression, and Ben was the recipient of the flood. She turned and, sobbing uncontrollably, ran off. Ben was too shocked to stop her.

"Ouch," he said.

"You deserved it," said Eleni.

"Ouch!" he said again, louder. "Well. Where were we?" And the thinker, the philosopher, Atlanta, unkempt, tie askew, socks down by her ankles, and not quite of this world told him.

"We, Ben, were and are beside the rhododendrons. But if you mean 'Where are we?' in a different sense then I would say that you are at the point of no return. Like, you know about Mallory and Irvine?"

"What you talking about, Atlanta?" asked Leo.

"Mallory and Irvine in 1924. Did they get to the top of Everest? No one knows. But they would have reached the second step, this last rock climb before the summit, and they would have said 'Shall we go on or shall we turn back?'"

"So?"

"So. They could've turned back, but once over the step they would've had to go on, too late to turn back."

"Well, what happened?" asked Alec.

"They found Mallory's body seventy-five years later."

"Where?"

"Below the second step."

"So did they make it?" Ben, at last, intrigued.

"I said. No one knows. But, do you really think they gave up after having come so far? No way. They went for it, and died trying."

"Well, I don't want to die."

"Ben," said Eleni. "This is not Everest. This is Stonegate."

"And it's not snowing," added Alec, but no one laughed. There was no snow, but there were other dangers lurking, lying in their path and Ben and all of them knew it. There were two frightening things happening both of which were really beyond their full understanding. There was the DVD, and possible involvement of the Headmaster himself. And there were the drugs which could involve criminals, real criminals. But this small group of friends were united, and, anyway, Eleni had already made up her mind.

"For Letty," Eleni said. "For all of us. Let's do it. Starting tonight."

21

Ben sat cross-legged on his bed. It was after midnight, it was pitch dark and, for once, he was afraid. An hour earlier he had crept downstairs and let Eleni in the double doors in the link corridor. She was in dark clothing, had tied her hair back and was wearing a grey cloth cap, pulled down over her ears. Still beautiful, he thought, despite the clothes.

"Don't follow me," she had said. "I know what I'm doing. Kretchner's first. That's easy. He leaves a key in the plant pot for his 'lady friends'. He's always away on Monday nights. If there's something to find, I'll find it."

"Eleni," Ben had said. "Be careful. I'm worried."

"Ben," she had whispered smiling. "I do believe you care!" His look had told her without words that he did care, more than anything.

"Look," she had said. "You have to go back. You know Watsham patrols with his torch. Any empty beds and we...no, you have had it. You must go now."

"Just...take care. I...you know." Eleni had looked at him in the dimness. There had been an eerie glow from the night lights, and deep shadows all around.

"Ben, this is the time. This is it." She had gently pulled him towards her. He had been shivering. She had held him and his arms had slowly and tenderly wrapped around her. In a way their movements were clumsy, their stance slightly awkward; neither had known physical intimacy before. But their innocent love, only intensified by the emptiness surrounding them, had been as strong and all enveloping in those brief seconds as any they would ever know. They had stood for a moment in the silence. Something deep inside him had stirred, and he would remember this closeness forever, her breathing, her gentle embrace, her head on his shoulder.

Then suddenly she was gone, moving silently along the corridor and up the cold stone stairs into the darkness above. And Ben returned quietly and sadly to his bed. He would not sleep until it was almost dawn and exhaustion would overtake him.

Eleni was more excited than frightened.

She felt she had nothing to lose in doing what she was doing, and she was used to wandering at night by herself. She knew Kretchner was away and if he did return she would see his car lights on the drive outside. She found the key, opened the door silently and closed and locked it behind her. The room was large and square. Being in the old part of the building it still had its dark brown, Victorian panelling round the walls up to head height. Above this the walls were painted a uniform cream. The bed was at the far end centrally under wide sash windows. There was a desk and a table to her left both covered with books and papers in fairly ordered stacks. On the right was a wash stand, and beside it was a computer station with all the right equipment and a large screen, at least twenty-two inches, she guessed. Pictures were few and far between, mainly dusty, faded prints which looked as though they came with the room. A dark, heavy cupboard and chest of drawers were on the fourth wall opposite the bed. There were no ornaments, no photographs. Not a family man, she thought. But his occasional women visitors seen arriving and departing at odd hours of the night had already confirmed this suspicion over the previous few years. He was not a man to mix with the parents, and only a few staff ever got past his door. One of those, Eleni knew, was Mr Luxmore on the night he had his accident.

Her heart was beating fast, but the thrill of the chase spurred her on. Put everything back how you find it, she thought; computer first. She would not be able to guess his password, that only happened in films. But she would turn it on, just in case, despite the light it would give off. She had a USB stick and several blank DVDs ready to copy anything exciting. She spotted a pile of CDs in the glow from the screen. Could be interesting, worth a quick scan. She heard a creek from the centre of the room, but the old building was always full of noises when the cold, night air got to work on the floor boards. The door was locked. She was alone.

With one last look round the room, she turned to the screen and started work. She had always been a hard worker, methodical and exact in her approach. This would be her toughest ever assignment. She worked for half-an-hour. The fear she had felt on first entering the room slowly faded as she became absorbed in her work. A pattern developed – load a CD, save it onto a blank disc, eject, replace, load another CD and so on. She did not waste time searching them online. That could come later. But there was something substantial on them as they took some time loading. She still had the USB to copy anything she found on the computer hard drive.

At last she was finished. She replaced everything as it had been, even allowing for the slightly untidy stacking of the CDs. Then she turned off the computer, stood up, crept silently to the door and left.

Where to now? She thought. There were other rooms to explore, offices, the sick bay with Matron's computer. She moved quickly; there was no point in wasting time and if she delayed there would be more chance of being caught. Matron's computer next, she thought, and hurried off up the short flight of stairs to the room that always smelt of witch hazel and soap. She drew a complete blank here. The computer was not working, and trawling through two hundred medical files was not going to achieve anything. All she found was a half empty bottle of whisky, but no doubt in Matron's mind it was purely medicinal. She left the room and headed for the staff room. This was a diversion because it was two floors below, but the temptation for Eleni of being able to invade the sacred space, the keep of the castle, was too great. She knew how to access the room by going down the back stairs past the domestics' common room. She arrived and, quite confidently, walked in.

The room was dark grey, lit only by reflected moonlight as it was at the back of the school. It was in a mess. Every available surface was covered with exercise books, catalogues, pieces of torn paper and other stationery. Two small tables in the centre of the room were crammed with empty beer and wine glasses, filled ash trays and empty cans of drink. Crisp packets and fragmented evidence of their contents littered the floor carelessly. There was a bar with an open ledger, a scrappy pencil dangling from it on a mangy morsel of string. The shelves had rows of cans and bottles, mainly alcoholic, and there were four upturned whisky and gin bottles with optics. The room smelt of stale beer, cigarettes and sweat. On the bookshelves were untidy, randomly angled piles of books and folders. Sports manuals were interleaved with old, worn dictionaries, cheap, heavily thumbed paperbacks, and various ancient Latin and Maths textbooks waiting for their long commuted death sentences to be carried out.

And all around the room was evidence of the true obsession of most of the staff: there were cricket balls, bails and scorebooks, team lists, a couple of scarred cricket bats, taped and bound. A few rounders bats and balls had dared to invade this predominantly male enclave, but were in a tight, embarrassed stack under a desk. Eleni shivered, not through fear but through an instinctive dislike for the thick, schoolmasterly atmosphere of the room, so redolent of men and women who were meant to care for the children in their charge, but did not. They were in a self-imposed prison, a retreat from the real world where they could indulge in their petty sports fantasies and reinforce them with alcohol and other hallucinatory substances. Children and any influence they might have were banned from the room, never being allowed to cross the threshold for any reason. Eleni smiled at the realization of where she was. But there was nothing else for her there, and she left. There was important work still to do.

Through it all she was undisturbed. She had found an open door here, a loose window there. And as she moved through the darkness stairs creaked, windows rattled, distant owls hooted. She explored the shadowy extremities of the empty corridors using her small torch judiciously, but went nowhere near the boys' dorms. To be caught there would mean instant expulsion. One or two doors along her way were locked; she had had to ignore those, however tempting. At last, tired but elated and satisfied with her night's work, she made her way down the main staircase. She was still wary of the darkness but she was content. She had gathered all she could and looked forward to examining it all with Ben's help, in the daylight. One more corner and there it was the link door, her way out of the building, with the low, slanting moonlight lighting up the opposite wall with a rectangular glowing patch.

Then she froze, catching her breath and sending a shudder of fear down her whole body.

Something...someone was standing in the shadows beside the door, watching her. It was a tall figure, not a child then, not Ben. It was unmoving but menacing. A voice, movement, a light turned on would have been bad enough, but there was something infinitely worse about the terrible stillness of the figure. She stood, petrified. All her previous courage had evaporated on the instant, sucked from her body. And then, in slow motion, the figure raised an arm towards her, just catching a beam of moonlight and lighting up its hand. It stopped, then made a slow but deliberate beckoning movement. Almost hypnotized by the outstretched arm Eleni took one faltering step forwards. Then she checked herself. Despite her terror, conscious thought was returning. "No!" she whispered to herself. "No," she repeated. She hesitated for a second, thinking rapidly.

Then she turned and fled down the corridor, absolute terror close behind.

169

22

The first thing Ben knew about Eleni's disappearance was when an agitated Alec shook him awake just before seven o'clock.

He had to be dragged from sleep and did not register what Alec was saying for several seconds.

"Wha...wha'dya want?" he asked querulously.

"Eleni, she's not there. Amy just texted me. She's gone!" Ben stared uncomprehendingly into Alec's animated face. Then he sat bolt upright in his bed.

"What do you mean 'she's gone'? She can't have. I saw her last night."

"I know. Not then. Now. She hasn't been in her bed since then. She's missing."

"No," said Ben. "Must be some mistake." He got up and started getting dressed. "Probably fallen asleep. That's it! Don't you see! She was so tired trawling through all the garbage in Kretchner's room she fell asleep there. That's it. We must find her before Vestey, or Kupp, or even Kretchner find her. Let's go." Before Alec or the others could react, Ben was at the door.

"C'mon!" he yelled, and ran straight into Matron, whose substantial figure was enough to cushion and then halt Ben's flight.

"And where do you think you're going, young man!"

"Sorry, Matron. Emergency. Got to go." He tried to squeeze past, but without resorting to physical violence he was going nowhere. "Please..."

"Now, stop, Ben! You are not going anywhere until you tell me what you are up to." Matron, angry and on home territory was not to be trifled with.

"Eleni, she's missing. I think I *know* where she is. I've got to go." Another failed attempt to get past the impenetrable barrier ensued.

"Now wait, Ben." Matron grabbed firmly by the wrists and held him, meeting his gaze. "What are you saying? If Eleni is missing how, pray, do you know?"

Confused, Ben became desperate: "I...just...do...Oh, damn it. Alec was texted by Amy, all right. So I know."

"Hey, Ben, thanks a bunch!" Alec complained. Matron held one hand out in a flash, and Alec walked over and surrendered the contraband reluctantly. "Sorry, Matron, meant to hand it in," he mumbled dourly. Ben saw his chance and rushed past, ignoring Matron's barked command to return. He ran to the internal fire exit stairs and ran, almost falling down one flight, out into the corridor and straight into the Headmaster.

"Ben Harrison!" he shouted. "Stop immediately!" Ben, momentarily deflated by the impact, stopped. "Where are you going, may I ask?" Head lowered, Ben resorted to mumbled monosyllables.

"Don't know, Sir."

"Not good enough, Ben. I think I know where you were going. Do you know where Eleni Fleming is?" He spoke deliberately and pointedly. He didn't like Ben and didn't trust him. The feelings, of course, were mutual. Ben looked up:

"No, Sir, I do not?" Then emphatically. "Do you?" "No. I don't. And if you do not go back upstairs, wash properly and then get dressed I shall lock you up, call your mother and send you home. Now go back up to your dorm." Ben backed away frustrated and angry. He was sensibly, for once, considering his options. But he was worried, almost panicking. He hurried back up to his landing, grabbed his wash bag and shut himself in the wash room before he could be questioned by anyone else. In the relative quiet of the room he was able to think while he washed and brushed automatically.

Where was Eleni? What had she done? She would not have run away. Not in her nature. She must be on site, perhaps asleep in some corner of a room. Perhaps she was outside, walking around the spinney after her night's work. Yes, that was it. She would turn up any second and the crisis would be over. Ben's panic levels subsided but a sense of unease persisted. Eleni had her head screwed on right (unlike me, he thought); it was unlike her to lose track of time or wander off unpredictably. It'll be all right, he thought to himself, she's fine. She will be there in breakfast at five to eight.

But she wasn't.

The seniors were abuzz with speculation and opinion.

"She never came back," said Amy, "after she left."

"I met her just after midnight," said Ben. "She went upstairs to Kretchner's room."

"Why?" said several voices at once.

172

"Doesn't matter," said Ben. "She just did. She's not there. They looked."

"Perhaps she got locked out. Couldn't get back in," practical Kirsty suggested.

"Well, why isn't she here now?"

"Perhaps she went to the sports hall. Fell asleep there, or the music schools."

"I told her not to go," said Sarah suddenly.

"When?"

"I met her on the way out. I went to the loo. Told her she was stupid." Ben, three places down from her, heard.

"Don't you call her stupid, you cow!" He half rose, threateningly.

"Cool it, Ben," said Joe. "She doesn't mean anything. It's just that all her wanderings don't achieve anything. What does she do it for? Some silly rebellion... A conspiracy theory," he added sarcastically.

"Not your damned business, Joe. If she wants to wander then she'll bloody wander."

"Well, she's asking for trouble then." Ben was about to erupt. Kirsty stepped in just in time.

"Look, you two, stop fighting. The priority is to find her. Stop bickering. Save it." There was general agreement. Kirsty often brought common sense to bear at times of crisis. "Watsham will say something at the end of breakfast. Let's wait for that." And, almost on cue, the Headmaster pushed his chair back, rang the small hand bell and waited for silence.

Twenty minutes later the desperate search for Eleni began. The police had not been summoned. Unlike with Letty there was no evidence that she had run away. It had been revealed to Watsham by Sarah

173

that she had gone for a wander in the night but that, she insisted, was all; there was at the present time no immediate need for panic. This was England, and if everyone kept calm and acted sensibly everything would work out.

But under the calm surface a nightmare was revealing itself.

Each one of the searchers held contrasting images of the missing girl in their heads: they could all picture Eleni, bright, beautiful, laughing, talking, running, her blond hair trailing in waves behind her. And each one also held the reverse image, the lifeless body, grey faced and still. But the search would dispel that terrible possibility – she would be found alive and well, they said.

And so they searched throughout the morning, under the early sun, the gathering clouds and then the rain that began to fall out of low speeding clouds. In scurrying groups they sped across the fields, clambered over fallen trees in the spinney, scoured the river banks. They searched and searched again, children and adults until, muddy, bedraggled and dispirited they crept back up to school to report their failure, to hope against hope that it was all a ghastly mistake, that she would be there to welcome them.

Ben, beyond exhaustion, had moved from hysteria to panic, from panic to despair.

Then Miss Peruzzi, firmly and with a clear tone spoke:

"Headmaster, you must call the police. You must call the girl's parents. You must do it now."

"Wait." Another confident voice spoke, Mr Cooper, practical, logical. "Before we resort to that I suggest we search the school buildings again. We panicked the first time. We need to search them room

174

by room, cupboard by cupboard, even drawer by drawer. What about the trunk room? Has anyone searched that?" Silence.

"Right, let's go." It was Mr Kupp's turn to take control. Whatever his shortcomings, he had been at the forefront of the search and had covered every inch of the fields himself. And off they went, calling, calling, voices echoing from dining room, corridor, classroom, dormitory. "Eleni! Eleni!" But there was no reply.

It was Twig Beech who found her.

He was in the library and while others searched behind curtains, under the librarian's desk, Twig stood in the centre of the room, disconsolate, lost in his own grief compounded by the unravelling tragedy.

"Oh, no!" he cried. It was a pitiful cry that froze the others where they stood.

"Twig," said Adeola, alarmed. "What is it?"

"I know where she is. The tuck cave. There by the fire. There! I know she is! She's there!" he yelled as he rushed to the panel and wrenched at it. At first it stuck, but his fingers gripped firmly and he pulled desperately at it again. Suddenly it cracked and gave way, revealing the grey, cobwebbed stone cavity behind. Mrs Woznak shone her powerful torch into it. Twig emitted a high-pitched, prolonged wail of utter despair.

Like a discarded, dust covered marionette, a sleeping angel, a grey stone statue, Eleni was half kneeling, her body wedged into the tapering gap back in the darkness between the two, rough stone walls. Her arms hung loosely, her tangled hair covering her face. Held up only by the cruel, cold confines of the cavity she was utterly still as though she had been there for a hundred years. There was no sign of life. Round her on the dusty floor were fragments of jagged stone. All that broke the greyness were patches, spots of reddy-black amongst the debris.

The small group in the library were stunned into immobility and silence. No one spoke for several seconds. Then Twig, terror overwhelming him, yelled once again: "Eleni!"

The noise ripped the others from their trance and Mrs Woznak took automatic control.

"Sally! Sally Garforth! Go, now, and phone for the police and an ambulance! NOW! Take Adeola. Get the Headmaster. Jeremy, get Matron. The rest of you get out of the library now." Twig didn't move. He was shaking, gasping for breath.

"Twig Beech! Get out, now!" Twig shrank visibly under the barked command, but did not move. "Go!" she repeated firmly. Twig still did not move.

"I can't!" he bleated. "I can't leave her. Don't you see – if she could get in there, so can I. I can reach her."

"No, it's too dangerous. We don't know what might have happened to her. There are rocks on the floor."

"Don't care. She might be alive, just hurt. I can reach her." He started towards the cavity.

"Peter Beech! Stay where you are."

"No, Miss." He shook his head, slowly, turned, bent down and edged forward into the darkness.

Faced with this utter refusal to obey, Mrs Woznak gave in. "Well, for God's sake be careful, Twig."

Behind him Twig could hear the library door opening and an influx of voices and bodies, but his mind was on the shadowy form of Eleni and the mounting terror of what might happen when he reached her." A voice he could not ignore though spoke out:

"Beech, this is Mr Watsham. You will tell me what is happening. Is Eleni all right?" Silence from Twig as he inched forward, staring into the dark. Light from the torch, still held by Mrs Woznak, lit up and then obscured the cavity as she tried to find the best angle for the bright beam.

"Answer me!"

"I...am nearly there. I can...almost touch her. She's not moving." He paused to wipe away tears and dust from his eyes and face. "I have got her hand." A wail of fear from Twig. "It's cold, so cold."

"Come out, now. You've done enough."

"Wait. There's somef...No, no, it's nuffing."

"What is it? What are you doing?"

But Twig only had thoughts for Eleni now. He realized that there was nothing else he could do. He released her hand gently. He looked up at her ghost like face for the last time behind its veil of dusty hair. "I'm sorry, Eleni," he whispered. "I'm sorry. I'll have to go now." Inch by inch he backed out of the cavity. As he neared the light his body was convulsed with uncontrollable shaking. Strong hands reached in for him, and he collapsed into the arms of Matron . He was dimly aware of a confusion of noises, echoing shouts and screams, a distant ambulance siren, footsteps, urgent whispers, his tightly balled fists, nails digging into his palms; and then he lost consciousness.

Under a copper beech tree on the edge of the playing fields was a circular wooden seat, surrounding the gnarled, ancient trunk. It was a favourite spot for people to sit on summer days. The sun had been out for hours now, and the seat was dry again, although the grass was still damp in places. Poppy, Atlanta and Henry were sitting there. The girls all liked Henry. He was quiet, polite, gentle, effeminate, the antithesis of the rugby playing prep. school boy so much admired by many of the staff. And he loved the girls, worshipped them from afar, but didn't feel he had to flirt or show off all the time as some of the others did. He was happy just to be with them.

Occasionally one or other of them would speak, but mostly they were silent, gazing out over the rolling Dorset hills, at the copses and fields and heath land.

What had happened that morning was so tumultuous, so far beyond their childhood experience that small, almost trivial details dominated what conversation there was.

"Buzzard," said Henry. "There. Look." He pointed high in the sky over the village. "And two more there." On cue, one of the birds emitted a harsh, cat-like 'Mew' that echoed around the valley.

"My shoe's wet," said Poppy. "Must be a leak."

"Girls' shoes are so flimsy," said Henry reflectively.

"Yeah, I know," said Atlanta, whose clothes and shoes were flimsier than most. "But...who cares?"

Another lapse into silence.

"She can't actually..." started Henry.

"No," said Poppy. "The ambulance took her away."

"We'll have to accept..." started Atlanta.

"No!" ssid Henry, quietly but emphatically. "Not until we know! Just don't say it!"

"All right," said Atlanta. "All right."

Peace again. Gentle wind stirring the leaves above them.

"Twig's gone home for the night," said Poppy. "Didn't want to. Mum just came and took him. Got here even before the ambulance. How do these parents find out things so fast?"

"Jungle drums," said Atlanta. Then suddenly: "We mustn't panic," she said. "We've got to hold it all together. Think about Eleni..."

"And Ben," said Poppy.

"Yes, and him."

In the distance, to their left, another car pulled out of the drive. Two more deserting the sinking ship, thought Atlanta.

"But, of course, it's all over now," she added.

"What is?" asked Henry.

"You know; all the trouble, all the plans, Ben and Letty, Vestey and Kretchner."

"Yes, s'pose so," said Poppy, sighing. "All over."

They felt strangely deflated, as though some great storm had passed. Even Ben had quietened down. When he was told about Eleni he didn't lose control, he simply stared blankly at the shocked messenger (a red-eyed Leo), went back up to his dorm and was found sitting there, on his bed after lunch, which he missed. He wouldn't eat anything and was left there, under the watchful eye of Matron. Ben's silence seemed to set the tone for the school. There was subdued conversation; the children walked in ones and twos. Younger ones, breaking into a run, would stop and walk, sensing that something was wrong, different.

But the calm was deceptive.

That night more blue and orange flashing lights were seen flinging their pulsating signals into the dark sky. There were no sirens, just the quiet hum of car engines and the silence of the lights. Then, as suddenly

179

as they had come, they disappeared, and the grey, monolithic school reclaimed the night.

23

At breakfast the next day there was still, obstinately, no news of Eleni.

Matron had fielded all questions with "I do not know anything. I have been here twenty-eight years, but I am not Senior Management. No one tells me anything." In the dining-room staff did not sit down, but stood in small groups, heads close, conspiratorial. Ben remained passive, but his eyes were fixed on staff. He refused to talk to his friends, and, discouraged, they eventually ignored him.

In assembly the tension rose, and even Kupp didn't try to silence the urgent whispering of the children and staff.

The Headmaster was late.

Five minutes passed, then ten. The noise level grew. Kupp sweated, loosened his collar, looked nervously at the side of the stage willing the Headmaster to appear. Then, without warning, he arrived walking quickly to his place behind the trestle table as the conversation died. The silence was palpable. All eyes were fixed on him. Ben clenched his fists until they were white.

"I am afraid," Watsham started, "that I have some very sad news to tell you." Sharp intakes of breath, suppressed sobs from around the auditorium. Someone said "No!" Watsham briefly looked up, face drawn and lined. He continued:

181

"Last night Danny Frampton, the assistant groundsman was found in the tractor sheds by the duty staff. He was unconscious. An ambulance was summoned immediately and he was removed to hospital. Unfortunately, medical staff were unable to revive him and he died this morning. His family have been informed. He leaves a mother, a sister and, I believe, several cousins. He was unmarried."

There was a stunned silence from the entire gathering. No one had expected this news.

"Before we remember Danny in our prayers and have a short silence, I have another announcement. As you know, Eleni Fleming went missing yesterday and was eventually found in the library. She was badly hurt and was also taken to hospital. The latest report from Dorchester is that she is still unconscious but is out of danger. She has a fractured skull and other minor injuries, but she should eventually make a full recovery." Like a pressure-cooker the tension was released. Expressions of relief and happiness filled the hall. Someone was crying. The name "Eleni!" could be heard from several places at once. "Eleni is alive!"

The Headmaster held up a hand for silence. "I should add that foul play is not suspected. The police have made initial inquiries and are satisfied that Eleni got into difficulties while out of bounds late last night. It is not known why she was in the main building. If anyone has any information about this incident he or she should come and tell a member of staff as soon as possible. Now, please bow your heads..."

Absorbing two such pieces of news at one time was hard for everyone. As they children poured out of assembly to go to their classes, there was a third piece of news. It was from Twig who had already been returned to school after a night at home.

"Luxmore's coming back!" an excited Twig announced. "I spoke to Mrs L. He's in a wheelchair. But he's coming back!" Letty grabbed him by his shoulders.

"Are you sure? Where...where is he?"

"I was off to my music lesson. And there she was, just going into her house. Mrs L smiled and sort of waved so I went to speak to her. She says a day or two, that's all."

Others then took over the excited questioning as Twig, the imparter of the good news, bathed in his moment of attention. Letty, though, slowly turned and walked away. She was happy, exceptionally so. Eleni was alive, Mr Luxmore was returning. She had her plan still, but events, mainly good ones were overtaking them.

She hurried off to her first lesson which was Chemistry. She liked Chemistry, but was a hopeless scientist. She treated it all as magic and this attitude ensured her continuing enjoyment of the subject, but equally ensured her continuing failure to pass any science exams. She had been put down a set for all the sciences, and was happy to sit in the back row and wonder at stars, electricity, chemical reactions and all similar miracles. She found herself next to Twig, and, within a few minutes the two of them were measuring and heating various chemicals on their Bunsen burner as the diminutive but strident teacher barked orders at them all. Twig was not his usual, voluble self and seemed preoccupied. Letty guessed what the matter was.

"Are you all right, Twig? What you did was very brave you know. And she's on the mend."

"Yes. S'pose so." He still seemed worried.

"Twig. It must have been a shock. Are you sure you're o.k? Did Matron talk to you?"

"Yes." Letty had the feeling that although he was being monosyllabic he really wanted to talk. They had to talk quietly and pretend that they were enthusiastically engaged in their experiment. Twig did the work to avoid the inevitable disaster should Letty become practically involved. She waited for him to speak.

"Letty?" he said, eyes glued to the thin blue flame of the burner.

"Yes, Twig. What is it?"

"Danny really *is*, you know, dead isn't he?"

"Yes, Twig, he is. Terrible. S'pose it was a heart attack or something." More gazing into the flame by Twig.

"No. Letty, I don't fink it was. I fink it was, you know, drugs."

"Are you sure?"

"Yes, I am. And I'm glad he's gone because he freatened me and I haven't dared say anyfing. Until now." He turned urgently to her. "Don't tell anyone, Letty."

"How did he threaten you, Twig?"

"Wiv a knife, Letty."

"Oh, my God! Why, Twig?"

"Because he was packing up some drugs, I fink, and I saw."

"O, Twig, that's terrible."

"And there's another fing. I don't know what to do wiv it?

"With what, Twig?" Twig looked sheepishly at Letty, then dug in his pocket and produced a small, blue USB stick.

"This."

"Where did you get it?"

"It was in her hand."

"Whose hand?"

"Eleni's."

"You mean when you found her? In that place?"

"Yes. Then." Letty gaped idiotically at him as she realized the possible significance of what he had in his hand. What had Eleni done that had resulted in her so called 'accident'? Had she found out something? If she had it could be on the USB. Who should she tell? The police had already failed her with the DVD incident. She couldn't risk that again. She had resolved to sort things herself, but she needed help. Whose? Mr Luxmore's? May be sometime in the future, but she needed help now. It had to be Ben and the others. It was up to them.

24

But Ben was preoccupied. Straight after assembly his mother had been waiting for him and got him straight in the car.

"What the hell do you want?" was his first question. His mother took the hit without a second's hesitation.

"I know, I deserve all that. I've come to take you to see Eleni. I've treated you badly. I'm trying to do something to make amends. Are you coming, or not?"

"Of course." And thirty minutes later Ben was at Eleni's bedside. And as he gazed at the white, damaged face of the only person he had ever really loved, he finally gave way to tears. Eleni's head was heavily bandaged. She had wires connected to a monitor that beeped annoyingly. She had a drip feed in her arm. She was in a deep sleep, drug induced. The doctor was "Optimistic", but said that Eleni had sustained considerable trauma from loose stone and brickwork that had hit her when she had dislodged it in her desperation to get away from her pursuer, if pursuer there had been.

He wept with the knowledge of what she had been through, the unknown terror that had induced her to seek refuge in that awful place. The stones of Stonegate had got to her and almost destroyed her. Even the building was against them. And he had let this happen. With his anger and guilt and

186

unquenchable desire for revenge. It was his fault, and there was nothing he could do.

His mother had the sense to stay outside the room. She was prepared for a long wait and was surprised when, after just ten minutes, Ben emerged and simply said, "Let's go." He didn't tell her how he had held Eleni's hand and how he had kissed her softly and tenderly on the lips. It was something he had never had from his mother, or anyone else. "Take me home," he ordered. And she did.

When it was dark Ben simply asked to be driven back to school. "Not until you've had something to eat," his mother said. So he pushed some hastily prepared scraps round his plate until she gave up and hurried him to the car.

They arrived back at Stonegate as it was getting dark. Ben asked to be dropped off at the gates. "Don't want to cause a fuss," he said. When she started to remonstrate he smiled and said, "Mum. I'm fine. I'll tell them I'm back. Just go home. And thanks for taking me to see Eleni." She didn't kiss him goodbye.

Ben waited for the car lights to fade, then set off down the road to the village. If he was spotted, so be it, but it was unlikely he would be caught. He walked and jogged down to the market cross, then cut round behind the houses down the lane that led to the church. A steep field finished by a low wall that went round the perimeter of the graveyard. Over that, then he was alone with the yew trees, an owl and a thousand silent gravestones.

He felt instantly at peace. The dead didn't argue, order, shout, interfere, betray, lie. They were past all that. Like the children in the church window – they were at peace too. He knew where their gravestone was and headed for it now. His torch spread a wide soft beam over the inscription:

In loving memory of
Alice Turnbull, aged 7
Who departed this life April 9th 1847
And her brother
Robert Turnbull, aged 4
Who departed this life April 22nd 1847

"Except ye be converted and become as little children
Ye shall not enter into the kingdom of Heaven."
Matthew 18.3

He extinguished his torch, moved back until he found the wall again and sat down in the deepening gloom. The outline of the church was silhouetted against the clear night sky, not oppressive but black and impersonal. It was not cold and he settled down and waited for some sign, for something to give him a lead. He had fought all his life against people telling him what to do, and yet now it was exactly what he most needed. He looked around him into the shadows. They were lit only by the faint, dying traces of weary, white starlight that settled gently on the field of the dead. But there was no terror here for Ben. In the blue-white stillness of the night there was a sense of lingering sadness left by the footsteps of the graveside mourners, whose flowers lay damp with dew, and already looked withered and neglected in the brooding shadows. He turned to watch the mournful moon like a limp and faded petal melt away as the first light wings of cloud drifted gently from the west, covering the star-bathed ground. Round him the shadows deepened, shrouded now in black night, and he was alone with the darkness around him and deep within him.

He lay down full length on the wall. It was hard but smooth and a covering of ancient moss gave it some softness in patches. He lost all sense of time. Eventually he fell asleep. He did not dream, but a sense of drifting pervaded his thoughts. He woke up once, stretched his stiff limbs, walked once, carefully round the church and returned to the wall. He slept again. When he woke for the second time the sky was lightening in the east. Time to move. He let himself gently down on the far side of the wall and half walked, half skidded down the dew-laden slope to the field below.

The dawn was dull and cold. Sinews of shifting mist infiltrated the hard furrows of the bare-backed field, and slid lazily down towards the dark stream that wittered fitfully in the shadows. One stark shape broke from the languid drifting whiteness and raised its grim presence from the frozen earth. The scarecrow stood like a decaying crucifix, mocking memories of the lonely church on the hill. Lank torn shreds of cloth hung like shredded skin from its emaciated torso, while its stick arms stretched handless like fleshless bones. The head, dark under its wilting cloth cap, drooped lazily on its hollow chest. And, in the shadow of its awful face, black eyes stared with mute accusation across the bleak earth at the approaching boy. Dead but not dead, blind but all seeing, silent but listening to the slow, heavy beat of the boy's heart, it waited.

Ben, grim faced and hollow eyed, stopped twenty yards short of this ragged figure. With all hope now extinguished, the future stretching ahead like a dark vacuum of despair, he felt not fear or loathing for this monstrous parody of life but a strange kinship.

189

"No hope, no purpose," it seemed to say. "Just give up. It's so easy to surrender." Ben agreed; neither of them had any purpose, any vision, any life left. He sank to his knees in the mud, cold, exhausted, empty. Was this where it ended, he thought? With victory for the bad people, the death, perhaps, of Eleni and, lastly, his pathetic demise on the damp, cold earth? He looked around him, at the slow creep of dawn, but saw nothing of comfort. Looming shapes of trees disappeared into the misty distances, still and indifferent to the kneeling boy. Nature was impervious to suffering, often caused it.

Then, from the invisible depths of the trees a sound rang out.

Three clear notes, repeated once. A pause. Then a sequence of four notes, followed by a rattle, also repeated. Again a pause, long enough for the sound to echo round the brightening hollow. Ben, distracted, looked up. Then a sound from behind him, an answering, rich whistle from a blackbird. A sudden, brief gust of wind stirred the scarecrow's rags, sent tendrils of mist swirling. More birdsong, from further away, answered by the song thrush, dominant on its high perch. Ben struggled stiffly to his feet angry at these interruptions.

"Shut it," he muttered quietly, then, "Shut it!" he yelled. But his voice echoed like a reprimand and he stood while the sublime, resurrected music of the dawn chorus rang in his ears. Ben, in a turmoil of opposing emotions, turned his back on the sagging scarecrow and stumbled slowly across the brightening field towards the distant school. Behind him a blackbird landed elegantly on the scarecrow's head, unaware of either the malevolent presence beneath its feet or the heavy heart of the boy disappearing into the last vestiges of the dissolving morning mist towards the dawn.

As Ben walked wearily up the slope he thought about what he had left behind in the graveyard. No, the dead didn't argue, lie and all the rest of it. Nor did they love, at least not in this world. And he still had Eleni. She was alive and so was he.

25

Letty had had a frustrating morning.

The USB stick, which Twig had willingly given to her, was burning a hole in her pocket. Lessons dragged on. English and Maths followed then Physics, and in break all the computer terminals were being used by queues of children disobeying orders and sending emails off round the known universe about the events at Stonegate. Then the duty staff cleared the rooms and sent everyone outside.

But at least the delay gave Letty time to gather a group together. Too many would draw unwanted attention; too few would run the risk of alienating trusted friends. Eventually she decided on Twig, Leo, Alec, Amy and Atlanta. They agreed to meet in the music schools after games. There were practice rooms with computer terminals there, and they should be undisturbed.

For once, games was something to be endured rather than enjoyed and at around five o'clock they dumped cricket and rounders bats and ran for the music schools, slowing to a walk as they approached to avoid suspicious glances from nosy staff and pupils. The six of them gathered eagerly round the screen as Letty produced and plugged in the USB. There was a brief delay when Twig complained he couldn't see, so Letty stationed him on the one chair. Everyone else stood, leaning forward in anticipation.

The USB contained four folders, all unnamed.

"Open the first one, Letty," said an impatient Alec as she clicked on it. The first one was an Excel document and consisted of several hundred pages of figures and what appeared to be sequences of closely related statistics. Many had what appeared to be compass bearings.

"What the hell is all that?" said Leo, mirroring all their thoughts.

"We want to know whose they are first," said practical Amy.

"Scroll down to the bottom, see if there are any comments or addresses." But after many pages of scanning horizontally and vertically the children realized that the numbers just ended, with no useful explanatory information to help them identify their source.

"Double Dutch," said Twig. "Scroll back to the top." Letty did so, and there they found their first clue. The file had opened several lines down from the top and on line one were, at last, some letters and words with more numbers, probably dates:

'EJK. 20/05. 2.00. David. Michael. Sandra 27/05.Poor. 1.00. David. Sandra. Colin. 03/06. 3.30 David. Robert. Damned street lighting. Handouts complete.'

"EJK!" Leo announced. "Kretchner."

"Yes, you're right," said Amy, "but so what? What are all those numbers?" They looked at the screen, baffled.

"Next folder," Twig suddenly announced. Letty clicked on the second icon. The folder contained a number of files, and it was soon clear that they were all staff files downloaded from the staff website. There was a password to get into it, but the children had known it for some time. When the Head of IT checked downloads at the end of the week, he would know exactly where they had been downloaded from and when unless they had come from a computer belonging to a senior member of staff of which there were several. They might only have three days.

"These look pretty random," said Leo. "Let's see what's next." Letty pressed on the third icon. Immediately pages of Word documents with Excel inserts appeared. Again there were dozens of pages. But the significance of these pages left the children gaping in disbelief.

"Oh!" said Twig, calmly.

"Shit!" said Alec, grinning.

"Party time!" said Leo.

The first page was clear, with explicit details about deliveries of commodities, distribution of the same, costs, payment methods, transport details, times and locations of meetings. There were details of amounts, dimensions of packages, methods of concealment, and many other facts and figures. It was a list of criminal activities and transactions, but it lacked two essential elements: there were no names, and no details of what the commodities were. And all the other pages were encrypted, or at least they seemed to be; everything was written in a mixture of letters, numbers and symbols.

There was nothing to say which computer terminal it had come from.

Initial excitement quickly subsided as they realized that there was not going to be any gift handed to them on a plate.

"Last icon," said Twig. They had forgotten about the last one. Attention returned as Letty clicked on it. It was a message from Eleni:

Hello, this is me. Hope you can make use of anything I can find. Am starting in Kretchner's room. Am in main computer room now. Will then go for random wander. It's fun walking around after dark. Not scared. By the way. In Kretchner's room found several unmarked DVDs behind the screen in blank box. No time to copy so took them out of box and hid them in animal hut underneath Kate's hamster. Very uncomfortable for hamster so: underneath his <u>cage</u> I should say.
Love, Eleni

They all read Eleni's message in silence. They were wondering what happened between her writing it and ending up almost dead in the library cavity. Something or someone must have terrified her. But she'd held onto the USB. Twig began to cry quietly. It was time to move.

"Let's go!" said Alec.

"No, wait," said Atlanta.

"Why? We know where they are."

"Yes," added Leo. "We know."

"Why are boys so stupid?" asked Atlanta, looking at the other girls. "Do you want the DVDs confiscated as soon as you get them? All six of us rushing into the animal room, apart from terrifying the animals, especially you Alec with your big gob is just what we do not want to do. I will get them. Then we will hide them until we have decided what to do. All right? Or shall we pursue your flash mob technique, Alec? Leo?"

"O.K., Atlanta, you've made your point. Just have to hope Hammy Hamster doesn't get a disk stuck up his arse before you get there."

"You boys are foul."

Five minutes later the friends were in possession of the USB and five DVDs. Despite temptation they agreed to hide everything back under Hammy Hamster's cage, including the USB stick. Hammy certainly wasn't going anywhere for a while. He would be the perfect guard, "But would probably," said Alec, "squeal under interrogation if caught."

The next morning Ben's dorm were surprised to find Ben in his bed fast asleep. He hadn't been there at lights out, nor had he been there when they stopped talking at around midnight. Matron was also surprised to find him there. She shook him awake and, ignoring the slightly damp earthy smell that wafted from under his duvet asked him how he had got there.

"Mum dropped me off last night. Didn't she ring you?"

"No, Ben, she didn't. What time was this?"

"Can't remember. Not too late."

"You should have signed in."

"Sorry, Matron. Forgot." Matron fixed him with a suspicious glare. Ben smiled back, innocence incarnate.

"Well don't do it again," was her answer as she took the path of least resistance. She had long ago given up trying to best Ben. She left the dorm.

"So where were you?" asked Leo, intrigued.

"In communion with the devil," laughed Ben.

"Not again," said Joe. "You really should get a life."

"Ah, but you see that is just what I have got," he retorted enigmatically. "And I intend to use it for various reasons."

In their form room after breakfast Letty and Alec told Ben about the DVDs and the USB. He listened with apparent detachment, but inside was making decisions.

"Yeah, interesting. Perhaps I could have a look sometime."

"Of course," said Letty, "but even we haven't seen the DVDs yet." At that moment as Ben looked casually out of the window, feigning lack of interest he spotted a man and a woman walking across the yard. He recognized them instantly.

"Gotta go," he said, and jumped up and was out of the form room before anyone could speak. Alec was first to the window and was just in time to see Mr and Mrs Fleming disappearing into the corridor towards the secretaries' office, closely pursued by Ben.

Ben in his headlong rush just managed to avoid crashing into them at speed. "Mr and Mrs Fleming," he said breathlessly. "Hello, it's me, Ben."

"Hello, Ben," said Mr Fleming cautiously. Mrs Fleming did not speak.

"Look, I'm so sorry about Eleni." He looked up. Mrs Fleming' eyes were red and tired. She looked down at the floor "How is she?"

Mr Fleming stepped forward.

"Ben. She is going to be alright...I think. But we can't talk now. We have an appointment with the Headmaster. We have come to thank Peter Beech for what he did."

"Oh, yes. Sorry." Ben hesitated, embarrassed. "Well, say 'Hi' to Eleni, please."

"We will." They turned, and left Ben standing puzzled and unhappy, in the corridor. He returned disconsolately to class.

With Mrs Beech's agreement the Flemings had been given permission to talk to the boy who had found their daughter. It was to be a private interview in the Front Hall by the main stairs. A member of the duty staff was stationed outside to ensure there were no interruptions. The Flemings were pleasant if unconventional parents. Like their daughter they were adventurers, seldom mixing with the Dorset county brigade, preferring to go abroad to places like Borneo and Bolivia, and back-pack. They were quietly spoken and lacked the starchily-dressed appearance of many of the Stonegate parents. They put Twig at his ease quickly, and, enveloped by the cushions of the Front Hall sofa he relaxed and started talking.

Mrs Fleming was tense, but managed to smile at the diminutive boy who had helped to save her daughter. But it was Mr Fleming who did the talking.

"So, Peter, it was very clever of you to find Eleni," he said encouragingly. "How did you know she was there?"

"Well...I s'pose it was the only place they hadn't looked."

"Why hadn't anyone looked there, Peter?"

Because they didn't know it was there. It was our secret store place. You won't tell anyone will you? It was where we kept food for feasts and fings."

Mr Fleming laughed. "Brilliant, Peter, or shall I call you Twig?"

"If you want." Twig beamed at this recognition.

198

"Well, Twig...by the way, why do they call you 'Twig'?

"Because I'm a small member of the Beech family and...I used to be skinny. Chocolate has changed things."

"Got it! Very funny. Anyway, Twig. I was thinking. If the teachers had known about this...secret place, do you think they would've found Eleni sooner?"

"Well, yes, of course. She would have been found before breakf... ." Twig stopped, realizing suddenly what he was saying.

"Yes, Twig, possibly. But I was thinking that if the staff had known about it, it would have been sealed up. Because as you know, it was a dangerous place, wasn't it."

Twig was trapped. What could he say?

"S'pose so." Mr Fleming leaned forward.

"Wasn't it, Twig?

"...Yes. It was."

"So, in a way, you and Eleni's other friends are slightly to blame for what happened, aren't you? Just slightly?"

Twig nodded, thoughtfully.

"So if you were able to help us work out what happened, you would want to help, wouldn't you?"

"Yes, of course. Yes," said Twig. "Anyfing." Mrs Fleming suddenly spoke up.

"If you know anything about what she was doing, anything about what happened, you must tell us. Do you see that?"

"Yes, Mrs Fleming."

"Do you know anything?"

"Well...yes. I do."

In 6A the first three lessons had come and gone relatively quickly. French was first and Ben had irritated Mr Kretchner by going to the loo twice. This was followed by English where they watched part of 'Of Mice and Men'. The third lesson was Art, where portfolios were being completed, and it was generally a free-for-all, controlled to a certain extent by Miss Peruzzi's strident tones and operatic interludes.

When break arrived it was raining, and so the Common Room was crowded and noisy. No one said anything when Twig came quietly in and sat down by the bookcases. A tennis ball flew in his direction. He pushed it away carelessly. Atlanta noticed something was wrong.

"Twig, Twiggy! What is it? Tell Auntie Atlanta."

"Nuffing. Just shut up!" was the retort.

"Ouch! Only trying to help."

"Well I don't need your help!"

Noise and activity continued unabated, but Atlanta, Alec and the other conspiritors exchanged uneasy glances.

They got their chance when the five minute warning bell for lessons went. As the others wandered off noisily, Alec, Leo and Amy came up to Twig while Atlanta kept watch at the door.

"Well?" Alec for once was not laughing. They all felt uneasy.

"You mustn't be angry," started Twig.

"I'll be bloody angry if you don't tell us what is wrong, *now*!" Alec continued. "Come on. It's time for lesson four."

"They made me, Eleni's parents made me."

"Made you what?"

"Made me tell them about the DVDs and the USB."

"Bloody Hell!" exclaimed Leo.

"So, what happened?" asked Amy, trying to be a little less threatening. Twig's bottom lip was quivering.

"I took them to the animal hut. There was kids in there, so I kicked them out. Then we moved the Hamster cage and got the DVDs but the USB was gone. We looked and looked. But it wasn't there."

"Stupid, stupid place to put it!" said Leo.

"You didn't say so at the time," said Atlanta from the door.

"Well I'm saying it now."

"And another fing."

"What now?" Amy asked wearily.

"When we got out Mrs Luxmore was there. She asked to speak to the Flemings, and waited until I had gone. Then they went to her house and went in."

Atlanta joined the group to hear the end of Twig's confession. They were not pleased with him. It was their discovery, their investigation. All of it gone.

"We are stuffed," was Leo's assessment.

"Not quite," said Ben's voice from the door. As they turned, he held out his hand, opened his palm and a small blue USB fell and hung, dangling from a long, looped piece of string.

26

The next day was one the children would never forget; it was Friday, their last Friday at Stonegate.

They would leave the school forever the following Wednesday. Talking about it later they never could get the sequence of events quite right. So much happened, so fast that it felt like a 'collapsing kaleidoscope' as Chloe described it.

But they all agreed that the first thing that happened was the argument about the newspapers. There were always newspapers on the table in the corridor, and they were usually well read. On this particular day however they were ripped to shreds before assembly. The Telegraph was the first to go, followed by The Daily Mail, then The Independent.

The children had never read about themselves and their school before in any national newspapers. And so when Harry Pugsley saw the headline 'Mystery Death at Leading Prep School' he ripped it out as a souvenir immediately. It was Danny's death (now officially attributed to a drugs overdose) that headed the articles, but Eleni's injury and hospitalization were also talked about, and tenuous connections were made between the two events. Others fought over the articles until three mangled piles of paper were all that was left. The children resorted to the television where the stories had failed to make the national news but were featured briefly in Television South West. In assembly the children were expressly forbidden to talk to any marauding journalists they might come across. Duty staff were instructed to remove anyone suspicious from the school site.

But it was half way through lesson three that the real excitement began. Jack interrupted a lecture by Mr Cooper on the legacy of the Victorians by standing up and stating in a booming voice, "My God, the fuzz are here in force! Look!"

The whole form, including Mr Cooper crowded to the window to see three police cars draw up outside the school. There were no flashing lights or sirens, and in fact not a single door opened for a full minute. Then suddenly all three cars disgorged a mixture of uniformed police men and women and three other women in everyday clothes. There were nine in all. Mr Cooper tried to restore a semblance of order. "Please go and sit down," he said wearily. There was no response until Kirsty put up her hand and said:

"Mr Cooper, Sir, there is something of possibly major importance happening out there which may affect us, you, maybe even the school. If we are good, please may we sit here and watch?"

Mr Cooper, sighed, hesitated, then nodded curtly and joined them at the window.

Two of the police men, one uniformed, one not, headed for the offices. The others stood by their cars looking up at the school, its windows and the eyes staring in wonder at them from all quarters. Then a uniformed policewoman casually detached herself from the group, wandered round the corner of the main building and disappeared from view.

"Mrs Luxmore! That's where she's going!" announced Adeola cheerfully.

"And why would you assume that?" asked Mr Cooper.

"Oh, no reason," said Adeola, with the sweetest of smiles. "Perhaps she's after a cup of tea?"

"Oh, dear God! You lot are a scheming, duplicitous, sneaky, manipulative bunch of adolescents. You are impossible."

"Thank you, Sir," said Chloe with genuine warmth.

Then a policeman took out a walkie-talkie, spoke briefly, put it away and gestured to his colleagues to follow him. They walked swiftly to the double doors and were soon lost to sight.

For two hours or so there was a strange calm. Nothing much happened, except lessons and break and lunch and all the other things that happen at school on a normal day. Everyone was waiting for something, but no one knew what they were waiting for. The whole school held its breath. Talking was subdued, spasmodic, hushed; conversations were started but drifted into inconsequential silence. Noises normally drowned out by many decibels of happy chatter were heard again – the swinging of the double doors into the school, the varied rhythm of shoes on tarmac, the drone and rumble of distant planes high in the summer sky. Then the bell went for afternoon lessons and the yard was empty again; but eyes were watching from every window. The police were still in evidence, but always in ones or twos, and they were relaxed and calm, drinking tea, munching dunked biscuits. The normality became oppressive. There was a high-pitched echo in the corridors as from the whistle of a boiling kettle, but it was always from around the next corner. Pressure was building somewhere just out of sight.

And then, movement.

204

A police woman appeared, got into a car, turned the engine on. Idled. The sound of doors banging, voices. Then the sudden emergence of two uniformed officers with a darker, hunched figure in between. It was Kretchner, hurrying, head down, ashamed, shamed. When he reached the car he looked up just once. He looked dazed, and very angry. He was helped into the car. Then it was off, no sirens or lights, just departure.

The school breathed again. And started talking.

Nine minus three leaves six. There were still three uniformed police and three other outsiders, possibly from the social services, on the school site. What were they doing? In 6A speculation was at fever pitch while they waited for Mr Cooper.

"I always knew it was Kretchner," stated a confident Twig.

"And what did you 'always know' about him exactly?" asked Joe scornfully.

"Well, you know, drugs and all that..."

"And all what?" Joe asked again.

"Leave him, Joe," said Kirsty. "You know perfectly well what he means."

"It's obvious, isn't it?" said Alec. "Those DVDs. It's porn, naughty man."

"Porn in itself isn't illegal. It must be really bad stuff if that *is* what he has been arrested for," Chloe added thoughtfully. "It could be drugs too. We know they've had some."

"So have half the county," said Leo.

"Not helpful," said Kirsty.

"But true," Leo retorted. "Look, the trouble is we do not know anything. Until we are told what's happened this is all guesswork." At that moment Mr

Cooper came in and there was silence. He looked quizzically at them.

"Well, one can only speculate about these things." He looked round the form sardonically. " And... about why on Earth Letty and Ben should be wanted by Mrs Luxmore. Go. You are 'required'." Ben and Letty hesitated, looked at each other, then back at Mr Cooper.

"Go," he repeated quietly.

Mrs Luxmore answered the door. She looked tired, but there was a strange expression, animated yet anxious, behind the eyes that both children noticed as they were ushered in to the hall.

"Thank you for coming, Ben, Letty," she said. "I...we wanted to talk to you. We thought it had to be you for various reasons that will make themselves plain soon enough."

"Mrs Luxmore," Ben started, "who is 'we'? she hesitated for a second.

"'We', Ben, is myself, Mr and Mrs Fleming, and...Mr Luxmore."

"Mr L!" exclaimed Letty. "Mr L!"

"Yes, Letty, it is. But you must understand that he is still not well. He understands everything, but his movements and speech are restricted. You must be patient. Now, shall we go in?" And they followed her into the drawing-room.

They hardly recognized Mr Luxmore. He was a hunched figure in a wheel chair. His head was down. He looked as though he was asleep.

"Andrew...it's the children."

And slowly his head lifted until he was looking at the children. His face was drawn and colourless and down at the corners of the mouth. He was obviously in

206

pain. But as he held their gaze a hand slowly rose and, trembling slightly, waved. Then his fingers, still shaking, clenched and turned; then his thumb rose. A thumbs-up!

"It's good to see you, Mr L," said Letty, smiling.

"Sit down, Ben, Letty," said Mrs Luxmore. They sat down and she said, "We brought you here because we thought there were some things you should know. I am sure there are lots of stories circulating already, so we want to tell you the truth. I think that Mr Fleming is probably the best one to fill you in." Mr Fleming stirred.

"Yes, thank you, Kirsty. Well, Ben and Letty; where to start? I suppose I should say, first of all, Ben, that I am sorry we almost ignored you when we met you in the corridor. We had just been to see Eleni, and we were quite frankly upset and tense. We know that you are very fond of her."

"How is she?" Ben asked.

"Improving, Ben, improving. But more of her later. First you need to know about yesterday." And he told them.

He had felt mean putting pressure on Twig to reveal his secret about the DVDs and the USB, but he felt he had to for Eleni's sake.

Poor Twig was terrified as he led the Flemings to the animal hut in case any of his co-conspirators saw him, but the hut was not visible from any classrooms so he was safe. They quickly located the DVDs but the USB was gone. Twig became extremely agitated at its disappearance and searched high and low, underneath all the animal cages and on the floor under the straw, but could not find it. The

Flemings, not wanting to upset him further, played down its possible significance, saying that they were very grateful for what they did have.

They left the hut and found Mrs Luxmore waiting for them. It was a fortuitous meeting. She had urgent news for them. Mr L., now at home, was still in a poor state. He could not speak properly, or walk unassisted. But his brain was functioning well. He insisted, in hastily scribbled notes, that the DVD he had found was Mr Kretchner's. They had had a terrible argument on the night of the car accident. Mr Luxmore had known that Mr Kretchner was involved in various unpleasantnesses and had accused him of drug abuse, drunkenness and other things to try to get him to give him information that might implicate others. He had failed. Mr Kretchner had resisted the interrogation. But Mr Luxmore had, against his better judgement, managed to pocket the infamous DVD. He had seen it secreted behind the computer, conspicuously separate from two neat piles of DVDs on the computer desk.

His suspicions had been right. He had examined the DVD in the privacy of his classroom and found it to be pornography of the worst sort, involving children. Highly illegal. So bad was it that he had decided to take it straight to the police, in the early hours of the morning. Then Danny struck. Was it a coincidence? Mr Luxmore had had time to think about that one. He thought not, but they would probably never know now Danny was dead.

The police now had the DVD, but the Flemings had five more. So they went with Mrs Luxmore to look at them. They dreaded what they would see, and their fears were confirmed within seconds of loading the first one. It was a product of depraved and truly wicked people; even the three, world-hardened adults were shocked and dismayed. They realized that they had saved the conspirators from seeing things that they should never see. That in itself had made their interrogation of Twig worthwhile. But the fact was that the children were in the care of an adult or adults who had been viewing these images. It had to be stopped.

The police were formal but very efficient. Initially suspicious of the Flemings, they quickly realized the importance the DVDs and officers of higher and higher rank were summoned until the weary parents found themselves in front of a Chief Superintendant.

The Flemings were sent home but by then they had gathered what was going to happen. A raid, quiet, low key, but carefully and thoroughly prepared, was planned for the next day. It had to be done during daylight hours because of the urgency of the situation. First stop was Mr Kretchner, but other officers went to inform the Headmaster of what was happening. The Flemings had come to school with the express intention of seeing Letty and Ben, but wanted to choose their moment carefully. So they stayed in their car until Mrs Luxmore came out to invite them in for coffee. They had watched the various comings and goings of the police, and one police woman who had come to see Mrs Luxmore was surprised and a little annoyed to find the Flemings in her house.

"This is not a public parade, you know," she had said.

The Flemings had acknowledged the intended rebuke, but told her why they were there – to see two of the children. Still suspicious, she left.

"So, I think you know the rest," Mr Fleming concluded.

"Thank you, I think we do, sort of," said Letty.

"Why, 'sort of' Letty?" Mrs Fleming interjected. "Is there something else?"

"No," said Ben. "I don't think so. I think that's it." He smiled a smile that failed to convince anyone present.

"Except for the missing USB," said Mrs Fleming.

"Oh, yes," said Ben with an unmistakably facetious tone to his voice. "I forgot."

"Ben, if you knew anything, anything at all, you would tell us, wouldn't you?" said Mrs Luxmore gently. Ben turned to her, smiled again, and lied.

"Of course, Mrs L." Letty was staring at him with fierce, bright eyes. But no one noticed because the doorbell went and Mrs Luxmore got up to answer it. Those in the room heard her open the door, and they could hear children's voices in animated conversation. They could not hear individual words, but something was happening. Mrs Luxmore then reappeared and behind her, flushed and wide-eyed were Twig and Kate. Mrs Luxmore, looking worried and puzzled spoke to the room:

"It seems that there are developments. Loud voices have been heard coming from the office area. Two policemen have emerged and are asking everyone to move away from the yard. Of course, this very action has had the reverse effect. Everyone is getting rather lively I am told."

"It's almost a riot," said Twig animatedly.

"It *is* a riot!" said Kate in a voice not far short of a yell. "I think it's a fight!"

There was an incredulous moment of silence from the assembled adults and children. No one quite knew how to react. What on earth was happening, they all wondered?

Twig broke the spell. "What are you waiting for? Ben, Letty. You must come. Now!" He turned and fled with Kate close behind, arms waving wildly as she ran, half tripping over door mat, flowers and paving stones. Ben stood up, breathing hard, as Mrs Luxmore, recovering, said:

"Yes, Ben, and you too, Letty, you must go. Quickly." Within seconds the adults were alone staring at each other in confusion tinged with alarm.

"Look, Mrs Luxmore," said Mr Fleming decisively. "I don't know what is happening, but I think we should find out."

"Yes, of course. Go1 Go! I will stay with Andrew."

It wasn't a riot. Or if it had been, by the time Letty and Ben arrived some sort of control had been restored. Several staff were out in the yard and Vestey with Kupp's assistance had calmed the crowd and subdued whispering was all that was audible under the barked commands.

"Now listen to me," Vestey said in his sonorous, grim voice. "The excitement is over. I want you all to disperse quietly to your forms. You will wait there for your teachers in an orderly and sensible fashion. There will be no..." But what there would be none of was never revealed as the double doors into the corridor swung open and Vestey and all present were silenced.

Through the door, looking distinctly wary, emerged a tall, uniformed policeman. He paused for a second then stepped aside to allow the ashen faced Mr Watsham to step hesitantly through onto the tarmac, followed by a police woman and a man who was obviously a plain clothes detective. Mr Watsham was noticeably shorter than his escorts but his bowed head visibly diminished him even more. None of them spoke. They started to walk towards the car park, slowly but purposefully. One small voice spoke above the silence. "Where are they taking him? Where's Mr Watsham going?" No one answered. The small procession continued doggedly on.

Then suddenly a commotion at the front of the crowd. Someone was pushing through. Someone stumbled and almost fell. "What you pushing for? Oh, it's you." A tall, slim girl whose moment had arrived appeared, and strode, head erect, to the front of the group, barring their progress. Watsham stared, uncomprehending. The girl stared back, fighting emotion, mouth closed in a tight line, her face almost level with his.

"Letty?" the Headmaster said, puzzled. Then without warning Letty lashed out with all her strength, slapping the face of the ogre in front of her with all her strength, all her pent up fury. The noise was like the crack of a whip. The leading officer leapt forward grabbing her thin arms. But Letty didn't struggle. Holding her head up high still she said aloud:

"That's for all the...that's for the times...that's for..." But then she found she could not speak any more. And Miss Peruzzi burst through the crowd, gathered the weeping Letty to her, wresting her from the confused officer.

Then everything happened at once. The leading officer grabbed Watsham by the arm and almost dragged him down the path. His colleagues followed close behind. The children, shocked, mouths gaping with sheer disbelief, turned to each other and back to the fast disappearing Headmaster, then to Letty and Miss Peruzzi who were moving quickly towards the staffroom. Vestey found his voice again and shouted "Move!" And within twenty seconds the yard was almost deserted leaving Vestey snarling at the stragglers and the dazed Mr Kupp standing, lost on the dark grey tarmac. He turned to watch the sleek white police car sneak smoothly out onto the road and down the hill. Habit caused him to look at his watch. Twenty past four, he thought, Monday. Time for Lesson 6.

27

Turmoil, panic, shock engulfed the entire Stonegate community.

The best view of the school during the twenty-four hours following the Headmaster's arrest would have been from one of the helicopters that regularly circled the school often hovering, sinking, rising, like damsel flies over a pond. It would have seen a succession of cars arriving, knots of people, adults and children, gathering and dispersing in seemingly random places. It would have seen some trunks loaded into cars as children were spirited away. It would have been witness to scurrying, hesitation, gesticulation, wandering, comforting, confrontation and other inexplicable movements. But it would not have been witness to hastily convened meetings by governors, staff and parents; it would not have heard the words, tirades, debates, gossiping, anger of a school in crisis.

And through it all the grey hulk of Stonegate remained unmoved, impervious to the strange noise and meanderings of its inhabitants. It would all resolve itself somehow. Stones that had seen two world wars, the passing of generations, would see life shake itself, adjust a little and then return to normal.

28

By Wednesday morning some things had resolved themselves; the facts were simple but momentous.

Mr Kretchner had been charged with possession of obscene material – the DVD that Mr Luxmore had taken from his room and the originals of the copies Eleni had made which had been found and hidden by the children. Under police interrogation he had revealed the source of the DVDs – the Headmaster himself. Watsham had prevaricated, delayed, obfuscated but had eventually cracked and admitted his guilt. While he was being lead away by the police his computer and all related material had been evacuated from the back of the school by the remaining police officers. As matters turned out it would have been better, Superintendant Claysmore decided, to have done it all the other way round – then the slapping incident would never have happened. Luckily but not surprisingly, Watsham was not going to press charges. Both Kretchner and Watsham had been released on bail with stringent restrictions attached; neither was allowed within ten miles of the school for a start.

That the school was still in crisis was not in doubt. Several parents had already taken their children away despite the best efforts of governors and staff to persuade them not to. The local press had had a field day, the nationals were investigating and South West Television had had a five minute report on the school and its woes. But the school struggled on. Staff and children tried to maintain a semblance of normality. There were sports heats to complete, tennis finals to arrange, reports to write. Kupp, Vestey and the experienced Mr Cooper rallied round and by enlarge the children were compliant. After a storm there was a period of calm. No one suspected that they were in fact in the eye of a hurricane and that worse was to come.

In Art during second lesson Jenny Peruzzi could not fail to notice the subdued mood of 6A. Letty had had her moment, but she was quiet, reflecting on the enormity of what she had done and slightly afraid of the consequences. The pervading mood among the rest of the friends was one of anti-climax, of something achieved but, for some reason they could not really determine, not yet complete. All they knew was that in two days' time they would be gone from Stonegate forever. They felt unsettled. And there was still no change with Eleni. She would be all right they had been told, but what had she still to say about that fateful night? There were still questions to be asked about Mr Luxmore's accident, and why Danny had suddenly given up on life and apparently killed himself with a massive drugs overdose.

And Ben still had the USB.

"Right! That's it!" Jenny's high-pitched voice cut through the silence. "Put your brushes down now. And , Master Beech, put that paint pot down immediately! You of all people should not be holding that. Put it down!" The form, mesmerized, stared at their teacher.

"We are going out. Not now. This afternoon. We are going up onto Woodsled Hill with a picnic. We will leave at two o'clock sharp."

"But we've got..."

"No, you haven't Kirsty."

"Physics is at..."

"No, Alec, it isn't. Not any more."

Revived spirits were further enhanced half-an-hour later, when they went into the village shop rather than going past it as they usually did on their Sunday trek down to church. There were fourteen of them including Miss so they were sent in in small groups to load up with goodies. They already had school supplies – Kupp had been only too glad to agree to the adventure and get rid of certain children for the afternoon.

It was only half a mile to Woodsled Hill from the shop, up a narrow lane and then quickly up to the top where there were glorious views of the surrounding country. The hill was a sandstone outcrop with centuries old paths crossing from side to side, end to end. Remains of human dwellings, and old walls gripped by gnarled tree roots gave it a mysterious but friendly atmosphere, especially on a day like today which was warm and still with white clouds like floating meringues casting light into the shadows.

They found their place, a little sandy hollow near the summit, and dumped their burdens on the soft ground. Released at last from the tensions of the previous days they played wide games, laughed and shouted, lost Alec and Amy again, found them, returned happily to their picnics. Their food finished, they basked in the afternoon sun on the peaceful hillside.

"I can't believe it's all over," said Henry, the first to speak for once.

"Yaay!" Kate exclaimed. "The goodies win again!" Her exuberance was infectious. Everyone was relaxed and happy. Twig was busily tunnelling into the bank. Chloe was happily ensconced in an enormous, dog-eared book. Alec and Leo chatted and laughed about their holiday plans. They briefly discussed the reason Ben had given for not coming with them all to Woodsled Hill. He'd said he had a headache, but he had said it with such lack of conviction that they were suspicious. But, hey! So What. It was more relaxed without him. Only Joe was quieter than usual. Usually the joker, he was aware of his less than honest behaviour towards the friends he had known for five years; Sarah had stolen his attention, Dog, his loyalty. But perhaps that was all in the past now, best forgotten before it was discovered.

It was Letty who saw Mrs Luxmore first. She had climbed onto the concrete triangulation point behind them and could see the small, delicate figure of Mrs L walking slowly towards the happy party, unaware of their presence. She jumped down.

"Hey, everyone, Mrs L is coming!"

"Where?" asked Leo.

"Just down the hill. She'll be here in two minutes."

Apart from Jenny Peruzzi, Mrs L was one of the few members of the Stonegate community that they were all glad to see.

"Let's invite her to stay and chat," suggested Kirsty.

"Could give her some food," Jack grunted.

"Haven't you eaten it all yet?" Alec asked. Sarcastic grin from Jack.

"Good idea." Jenny Peruzzi stood up to get ready for Mrs L. "She can sit there. Amy, Alec, stop

218

that and move please." With embarrassed grins the two lovers got up to vacate the place where a grassy bank formed a natural seat. "Poppy, Letty - scavange for food. Twig, go no further into the bank or you will probably the first mining casualty on this hill in a thousand years."

As Mrs L came within view the group spontaneously arose to greet her.

"Hello, Mrs Luxmore," they said with genuine warmth. Mrs L, mildly startled, soon recovered her composure.

"Hello, children, Jenny. What *are* you all doing here?"

Jenny explained: "on day release from prison, basically," she said. "Come and join us." And so Mrs L sat down with them and a half hour that none of them would forget followed. News of Mr L was all good. He was recovering use of his arms and legs, he would be "Off round that spinney again soon," and, most important of all, his memory was returning. And he could laugh without it hurting.

Eventually, Mrs L got up to go. Her final words were to all of them. "Tell Ben when you see him to look after Eleni. She is a brave girl. She took on what my Andrew could not finish. And all of you, look after each other. You should not have had to go through all this. Goodbye, and thank you all for tea." As she disappeared from view the children were quieter than before. Henry, with his usual insight, voiced what they were all thinking.

"It's not over, is it?"

"No," said Twig. "It isn't. I don't mean the Kow Klub, I mean everything else. Like Eleni, Vestey, drugs and fings." No one else spoke. They were divided between those who didn't want to think about it and those who were still haunted by it. They all still felt uneasy about Ben, but no one mentioned him, no one wanted to spoil the moment which had so cleverly been created by their sympathetic art teacher, Jenny Peruzzi.

And Ben did not have a headache. Ben was in euphoric mood. He was alone in his classroom and was staring at Mr L's computer screen. He did not have any passwords so could not break into anyone's site. He didn't need to. He had plugged in the USB and was scrolling its contents. There were hundreds of pages. Many were just a vast jumble of apparently indecipherable symbols. Occasionally there was a date, or simple initials and, oddly, one or two isolated comments such as, "Yes! Yes!" or, "Stupid!". One whole page just stated in bold capitals, "THIS IS THE ONE." The words stared out at Ben challengingly. What "one", he thought?

Who *are* you?

He had trawled through more than a hundred pages of symbols, spaces, gibberish when suddenly he struck the gold he had been seeking. There were lists all programmed into an Excel spreadsheet. Dozens of them. There were initials to begin with, no names, just initials. Then there were dates, and times. And when Ben pressed on any one of them further sub-lists were revealed, and this was when frustration gave way to his new euphoria. Coke, it said, three kilos. And then the words cascaded onto the screen: marijuana was mentioned, coke again, several times. Weights, times, strange numbers: map references? More numbers, dates, initials. Then heroin, amphetamine stared out at him, then hashish, ketamine ("What's that?" he thought), and these were followed by weights, more dates, strange symbols and more numbers, more initials. The dates, if they were dates, were from up to five years before and ended in May.

Ben's heart pounded inside him, he felt a surge of power swell inside him as he began to realize what he had found. This was the big one. However disgusting and foul the DVDs had been, this dwarfed them all.

Ben was only thirteen. Only thirteen. But he was old enough to know about what drugs were doing to the world, to the addicts that roamed the city streets, to the Columbian peasant farmers, the Afghanistanis, the Mexican villagers, his mum. The children had been told all about it in current affairs lessons. And someone at Stonegate was in it up to his, or her, neck. Who was it? Danny had been in it, but he was a mere minion and had died because of it. Mr Luxmore! The thought suddenly struck him that Mr Luxmore had been hit by Danny. Maybe his accident was nothing to do with the DVD, more to do with worse things – he might not have even known what he was interfering with. There was a rotten world at the heart of Stonegate, the whole place was infected and it was being held together by ignorance and apathy. And when someone innocent got hurt the school just turned its back and continued as if nothing had happened. Ben felt alone, but didn't care; if anything he felt stronger.

The thought occurred to Ben that he should go to the police and give them the USB, wash his hands of it, be at peace at last. But he knew he wouldn't. For Mr Luxmore's sake, for Eleni's sake he had to do this himself. And if it all went wrong, well, he would probably not survive and who would care about that? He took the USB out of the computer and shut it down. It was time to go.

His mood had changed again. He felt the blackness return. But with it came calmness, and a resigned determination to carry on.

29

Ben was tired. It had been a long day and confused emotions tumbled around in his exhausted brain.

The arrest of the Headmaster had been an event beyond his wildest dreams. But somehow he felt cheated. Vestey, the architect of his woes was still at large, and thriving, it seemed, on the chaos around him. He had emerged stronger than ever from the recent events. And Cupcake – the idiot – was still at large, utterly harmless may be, but still there. And worst of all was what had happened to Eleni. He looked at her now in her hospital bed. Her pale face was still coloured in patches by the bruising she had sustained. She was still attached to tubes, and machines that beeped. She was still very, very ill. And she had things to tell him, anyone, when she regained consciousness. What had happened to her? What had terrified her so much that she had fled to that terrible little stone cave, almost, thought Ben, her mausoleum? Wake up, Eleni, wake up. Tell me what happened. Who did this to you?

As if in answer to his silent pleading, Eleni's eyes began to open. Just a fraction at first, but there was definitely movement.

"Eleni!" Ben said urgently. "Eleni!" His heart almost burst with disbelief. Her eyes closed again, but her hand twitched, an almost imperceptible motion. Gently he reached out to her, softly enclosing her cold hand in his. A squeeze! Just a minute pressure, but a squeeze!

"Eleni! Can you hear me?" Another squeeze. "Oh, thank God! Eleni, I am here. You are safe. You're going to be all right!" He was frantic with the urgency of the moment, the desire to communicate with this girl. He remembered, almost felt physically, the sensation of their last contact in the corridor, the night she had gone on her last expedition. But he had to be careful: Mr and Mrs Fleming had only left him alone with her for a few minutes. They could return at any moment, and he wanted time with her alone.

She opened her eyes again, just the merest fraction. Her lips moved. There was no sound, but "Ben," she mouthed, "Ben".

"Yes, yes. It's me. Your parents are here. You're safe. Twig found you. In...that place. You were hurt."

"Twi...," she mouthed. "Twi..."

"Eleni. Can you remember just one thing? Just one?" He leaned in close to her. "The USB. We have it. Eleni, where did it come from? Whose is it?" Eleni's eyes closed once more. She was absolutely still for several seconds. Then Ben was suddenly aware that Eleni's parents had entered the room and were standing behind him. He turned.

"Ben," Mrs Fleming whispered. "Is she awake? Is she conscious?" She moved quickly to her daughter's side.

Ben nodded. "She was, Mrs Fleming, she was for a second."

"Did she say anything, anything at all?" Her eyes were full of concern and fixed on her daughter's damaged face. She hardly heard Ben's answer.

"No, Mrs Fleming. She didn't. She's asleep now." He stood up. "I need to get back to school now, if that's all right. Thank you for letting me see her."

"That's fine Ben," said Mr Fleming. "It's the least we could do. Perhaps if you go and wait in the car now, we'll just spend a minute or two with her. Say goodnight. Is that OK?"

"Of course. Is the car open?"

"Yes, Ben. Lock yourself in if you want to. Here's the key." Ben caught the key and turned immediately down the long, brightly lit corridor. His thoughts were racing, but paramount in his mind was the wonderful feeling of having seen Eleni open her eyes, of seeing her trying to communicate. He would treasure those brief moments.

Back in the car he sat and thought. What should he do next? He felt tired, but knew he had to see things through to the end. Eleni had not told him where she had downloaded the USB from, so he had to find out himself as he had already planned to do. But a great weariness was washing over him. He wanted more than anyone for it all to be over, the term, his five years at Stonegate, and the blackness that oppressed him almost every waking moment.

He sat still for several minutes. The Flemings were taking their time. Perhaps she had woken up again. The minutes passed. It was still light but a hazy gauze had drifted over the sun and anyway Ben was hidden from its pale light by the bulk of the hospital, which was grey, square and several stories high. He sighed. Then something made him turn and look across the car park to the hospital doors. It was the Flemings! At last! But just as the automatic doors opened they stopped. Mr Fleming put his arm round his wife's shoulders and seemed to whisper in her ear. Then

225

slowly he lowered his arm, and she turned towards Ben. Too far to see his expression. She started walking, leaving her husband in the shadow of the door. Her pace was hesitant, her head lowered as if she was thinking. Then, with ten paces to go she looked up.

And Ben knew immediately.

Their eyes met. Mrs Fleming would never forget the face she saw. She couldn't hear Ben's cry of anguish, but she saw his face fall apart, she saw his desperate hands pressed against the glass pushing her away, refusing to acknowledge what she had to tell this poor, haunted boy, the thing that had ripped his heart from his body moments before. She hurried the last few paces and wrenched the back door open. Ben backed away into the far corner moaning as his contracting chest squeezed breath from his body. "No!" he managed to whisper. "No, she..."

"Ben, Ben, listen to me. Eleni's alright, she's alright. It's just that she had...there was a problem. An emergency." In the face of Ben's terrified face Mrs Fleming herself began to lose control. She stared at Ben, eyes filling with tears. Then she pulled him towards her and held him tightly almost violently as she just managed to gasp out the words, "They got her in time...revived her. They think...they don't know, but...they think...She's got a good chance, Ben." Ben gazed past her shoulder and saw Mr Fleming slowly turn and walk back into the hospital. Even at that distance he looked broken. Ben sighed, dropped his arms loosely to his side.

"What happens now, Mrs Fleming? What do we do now?" Mrs Fleming pulled back, puzzled, drying her eyes.

"What do you mean, Ben? We...we just have to wait and see..."

No, I mean now. Where do we go now?"

"Oh, I see. Well, Ben, I'll take you home, to your Mum. She'll be worrying." Ben looked past her into the shadows of the grey hospital walls. What did he want? He felt so numb with loneliness, pain and disillusion with his whole life that the future seemed to be a blank page, a void. But a decision had to be made, and as he thought of Eleni he turned to Mrs Fleming and said the only thing he could say:

"No," he said with a strange determination returning to his voice. "No, Mrs Fleming. I would like to go back to school, please. I want to go back to my dorm."

Ben couldn't ever remember the journey back to Stonegate. But by ten o'clock he was back in his bed with his eyes wide open in the darkness. He could hear subdued catches of talk from the matrons' sitting room. So they knew did they? They knew about Eleni. Ben looked through the curtainless window. It was dark and there was no moon, and wafer-thin high cloud dimmed the starlight. No one was asleep in dorm, but Ben was not in the mood for talking to anyone, neither his friends nor anyone else who may have been watching over him. He had plans, and would wait until the early hours if necessary before moving. And he had lots to think about.

He knew he was on his own now and that he had to finish it all himself.

Eleni was the only person who filled his mind, but he knew that she had cared about everyone else, not just him. He did not and, although Eleni had influenced him, had changed him for the better, he had something to do before he could turn back to her. He was aware of his own antisocial attitudes but could not do anything about them. Or would not. Of course, because he had been labelled The Bad Boy, The Rebel, he was popular; everyone liked him, or said they did. He was cool, mysterious, a little frightening. And he played on that. It wasn't difficult. He really didn't care what happened to him. If you drop beneath a certain level of self pity and depression you reach catharsis without realizing it and then you cease to care about yourself and anyone else. And Ben had reached that low point a long time before.

When?

Was it when his abusive father had left home? Or was it when his mother started having "boyfriends"? He really didn't know. But when your emotions became dulled and blunted time ceased to have meaning too. And the world was just...the world. There was no wonderful, intangible love, no great, unsolved mystery, and if God was up there he was not communicating very well. The blackbird's song that had so enthralled him as a young child, as it echoed its heartrending sound round the houses, was just a series of meaningless, random notes now. What about friends? Nothing, really, just mutual support systems in a rotten, crumbling world.

And then suddenly there had been Eleni.

He had tried to be offhand with her, show her he didn't care, avoid her eyes or, if she caught him unawares, grin stupidly, put up a mask of indifference. But it didn't work, not for a moment. He was smitten, rendered wobbly at the knees whenever she appeared. His years of coldness made it possible to hide his feelings, keep them frozen, concealed inside his deep frozen soul. But every day he had felt the drip, drip of ice thawing, and there was nothing he could do to stop it. Eleni's pale face in hospital, her cold hand, the tears just made the ice melt more quickly. And now she was on the edge of an abyss. And if she fell, if... . A wave of terrible realization swept over him and threatened to drown him and leave him cold and desolate but he fought it off with almost physical force. Later, he thought, later.

So now he had to finish what she had unwittingly started. He had the USB; and he was convinced that its content made the DVDs that had done for Kretchner and Watsham pale into insignificance. He knew it because Eleni had nearly died trying to escape with it, because the whole rotten edifice of Stonegate was ready to crumble and the USB was the tiny stick of dynamite that would start the collapse. But who did it belong to? Who was the monster at the heart of it? He hoped with all his heart it was Vestey, the man he hated beyond any other, but it could be anyone. Eleni had roamed the school on that night – there was nowhere she might not have gone. Ben had to light the fuse that would cause the explosion.

"Here we go," he whispered to himself. The dorm was now silent except for some rhythmic, heavy breathing. It didn't even need a conscious decision, he just got out of bed, donned track suit and trainers and was out of dorm within seconds.

Where the newer buildings containing the dorms met the old monolith of Stonegate there were some architectural oddities. There were strange little stairways and corridors, cupboards and hatches, windows with brick walls behind them. And just

229

beside a small store cupboard in the matrons' wing on the top floor was a ladder attached to the wall.

Ben was standing by it looking into the darkness where the rungs disappeared upwards through the low ceiling like in a submarine conning-tower. He clambered clumsily up, swaying from side to side, the large wooden encumbrance in his right hand obstructing easy movement. His head bumped hard against the hatch at the top, but adrenaline pushed the pain away as he pushed it open. A sudden rush of wind swirled up past him as the warm air trapped by the hatch rushed into the night above.

He quickly hauled himself up and found himself on a small, lead platform with the steep, tiled slopes of the roof slanting off in the cold moonlight. Everything was grey. The lead, the tiles, even the stone was monochrome in the misty night air. Ben felt this was his world. He was not afraid of the dark, of the dangerous drops that lurked almost invitingly on every side. He felt relaxed, calm. He smiled to himself in the darkness. This is where it would all play out, he thought, one way or another.

He tested the roof tiles. They were dry and firm; his trainers gripped well as he began to climb. Five steady steps and he was gazing over the top into the mist-swathed distance. Lights winked from farmhouses, there was a glow on the horizon that could have been Dorchester. And there was silence except for the gentle, occasional flap of the school flag on its pole away to his left and down by the rhododendrons. He carefully sat astride the roof, caught his breath, looking round at his new dominion. Then he started moving backwards, hitching himself up and back, six inches at a time, still with the wooden burden gripped tightly in his right hand. He mustn't drop that, that would spoil things. The shadowed rectangle of the vast central chimney stack loomed up behind him. He paused again, then moved into its shadow until he felt the cold stone ease into his back. He leant luxuriantly against it, let its strength support his aching muscles, closed his eyes. But now was not the time to relax. A sense of urgency returned.

He opened his eyes and felt behind him for the lead-lined gutter that joined onto the flashing at the base of the chimney. There was a corroded copper wire too, the lightning conductor. It was loose in places where metal pins had come away from the crumbling stone. Perfect, he thought, and did what he had to do. Within seconds it was sorted and he was hitching his way, unburdened now, back along the roof.

He reached the hatch, paused briefly to look back at the grey, cold world he had discovered, then disappeared back into the bowels of the building.

30

The common room was more crowded than usual. It was the last full day of their Stonegate lives and they had congregated naturally in their favourite place. Every chair was overloaded and sagging, even the beanbags had at least two occupants each and a few others were sprawled carelessly on the carpet. Chloe was on top of her favourite bookshelf. A tangibly subdued mood suffused the room where even the large Caribbean mural looked paler as the paint peeled in dusty silence from the plasterboard. The chatter was spasmodic and inconsequential as Leo twanged desultorily on his guitar strings. Jack spoke up, his broken-voiced growl getting everyone's attention:

"What time's the barbecue?" He was thinking about fat beefburgers sizzling on the grill.

"Seven," said Kirsty. "It's always seven. Then a swim at eight-thirty. The film's at ten."

"Seen it before," said Kate, "three times at least."

"Well you obviously like it then."

"I do. I'm not complaining. I'll watch Johnny Depp a hundred times if I have to!"

"Crazy Kate," commented Alec pleasantly.

"You coming, Ben?" It was a tentative but genuine enquiry from Poppy. She had noticed Ben, lost in thought, sitting in the corner of the room by himself. He looked up and, forcing a smile, replied,

232

"Think I'll give it a miss actually, Poppy. Got things to do."

No one asked what it was he had to do. Many of them guessed how he must be feeling, with Eleni in hospital, and lots of other torments, large and small, whirling round in his mind. Of all of them he was the one who was the implacable enemy of the authorities; the one who, even when leaving Stonegate for the last time, could not make peace with an institution that had in one way or another rebuked him, humiliated him, punished him for five years without having bothered to understand him or help him in any way.

Having his friends gathered around him now gave him more comfort than they probably realized, indeed they were his *only* comfort. The sweet smell of sugary confectionary that filled the room held no attraction for him although he couldn't restrain a wry smile at the sight of Twig Beech in seventh heaven as he bit into his second Cream Egg of the morning break. He, thought Ben, had absolutely no idea what was about to happen.

Neither do I, he reflected. But I know what I want to happen.

And with that he knew the time had arrived. He struggled stiffly to his feet. He looked at Leo and Alec who were absorbed in some undoubtedly scurrilous gossip across the room. "Alec, Leo. I wondered if I might borrow you for a minute?" The addressees were a little perplexed for a second – Ben had never been so polite before. And he seemed tired, and a little tense, under the apparently calm exterior. "You coming?" he queried.

"Yeah, of course, Ben," said Leo. Alec said nothing but got up anyway, raising his eyebrows in response to the questioning eyes that followed the Ridicules out of the room.

"Where're we going?" Leo asked. "What's up, Ben?"

"Just want a little favour, if it's okay."

"Yeah, sure. Anything." The Ridicules had reached the top of the stairs, but suddenly Ben stopped, turned and faced them. He stared at each of them in turn before bringing a small, padded envelope up into their line of view.

"I," he started slowly, "have a little package to deliver."

"To who?" asked Leo.

"To whom?" corrected the pedantic Alec.

"Well," Ben said with a smile. "I don't really know. That is the point."

"Don't get it," stated Leo flatly.

Ben paused for a moment. His smile disappeared and when he spoke next his tone was like ice.

"I have here a little item I am returning to its owner. It is a USB stick – yes, *the* USB stick. I am going to hand it into the staff room with a note attached. Eventually, I hope, the rightful owner will appear to thank the person who handed it in. I want you two to lead him to me." Ben stopped talking and waited, eyebrows slightly raised, for a reaction.

"Well, yeah, of course we'll do it," said the ever loyal Leo. But Alec was suspicious.

"What's in the note, Ben?"

"Need to know basis, I'm afraid," Ben said casually. "But basically it says 'To whom it may concern, one USB stick, slightly used, a present from Eleni Fleming.'"

"Christ, Ben!" Alec exclaimed.

234

"What?" said Ben innocently.

"You know bloody well what. That stick is stuffed with things that should be with the police. It's far worse than those DVDs and you're absolutely mad to play games with it." But Ben was already shaking his head.

"Not listening. Not listening. If the fuzz deal with it you know what'll happen – possible arrests, lawyers, delay, everyone knowing who's guilty and then he escapes on a technicality and Eleni and Mr L hurt or worse for nothing. Not going to risk it. Sorry." The other two stared at Ben. They were angry but had nothing more to say. They knew Ben was unmoveable and that there was no point in arguing.

"You're crazy. I should tell someone about you," Alec said lamely.

"I agree," said Ben. "But you won't."

"I know," sighed Alec. "What about you, Leo?"

"Well," said Leo reflectively. "I don't like it either. But I suppose this is what the Ridicules are for. It's been leading up to this, hasn't it? So...what are you planning?"

"Best you don't know..."

"I knew it!" said Leo.

"Something stupid..." Alec added.

"May be, but easy for you," Ben said decisively.

"So what is it?"

"You just need to point Mr X in the right direction, that's all. When he comes looking for me, I want you to be awfully helpful for once, and make sure he finds me."

"So where will you be?" Alec asked. And by the time Ben had told them, they were even more convinced that he was mad, but loyalty to the cause prevented any argument or even discussion, and they reluctantly agreed. It was going to happen after lunch, in rest, when the whole school were in the Theatre, reading.

At exactly ten to two Ben went up to the staff room door and knocked loudly. The door was opened almost immediately by Miss Garforth who, unusually for her, seemed distracted and angry. She was short with Ben.

"Ben, what do you want? You know you should be in rest, and there is absolutely no need to knock so loudly. Now, what is it?"

"So sorry," Ben said with a smile. "Just wanted to return this. I think someone here is missing it rather badly."

"What is it...?"

Ben thrust the envelope containing the USB and note into her hand, turned and fled.

"Ben," she called, but he had gone. Shrugging her shoulders, Miss Sally Garforth closed the door, turned and opened the envelope. She took the note out, read it and called out to the ten or so staff in the smoke filled room. "Sorry everyone! I have a message for you all. I have a note which says 'Dear Staff, if anyone is missing a USB, or information thereon...'"

Ben sat in the cool breeze, high up above the school. He found it hard to focus. His subconscious was trying to persuade him that everything was fine, that he was just a boy, in a slightly unusual place, watching the clouds pass by. But his conscious thoughts were in turmoil and he was starting to panic.

Perhaps Alec and Leo were right – perhaps he was mad.

And perhaps he was about to die.

Suddenly he realized that although he did not care about being dead he definitely did care about dying. The image of a rampant furious Vestey coming at him across the roof terrified him. He would be flung like a rag doll off the roof and there would be one second of unimaginable terror before oblivion saved him. There was still time to change his mind, he could reach the hatch, drop down the ladder and run. He pulled away from the chimney. Stop this foolishness, he thought, get to safety. But, cutting through his panic to the terror beneath, a loud voice, muffled but powerful and angry, could be heard booming up the hollow tube beneath the hatch. "Where is that little bastard! This is the end!" Coming from down below him it sounded to Ben like a voice from Hell. So it was Vestey after all. He was right.

Then the hatch slammed open and the furious head of Vestey appeared. Ben froze. Vestey, blinded by anger, took several seconds to locate Ben against the grey, chimney wall. When he did his mouth opened, his eyes dilated. Ben braced himself for the noise that would engulf him. But Vestey's outburst never came. Instead, a quieter voice, steady but full of quiet authority came from below him.

"Mr Vestey, I must insist that you come down at once. You must leave this to me." The voice, from twenty feet below the hatch and dulled by Vestey's bulk, sounded strange. But Vestey's reaction was almost immediate. With one last angry glance at Ben, he looked down and said "Yes, right...of course." Then he disappeared from view. For some seconds Ben was left in peace again. The wind whipped gentle, teasing

237

tendrils round his exposed body and face. Then Ben could hear the faint, metallic sound of shoes on ladder. Brief silence. Then a head slowly appeared.

31

Mr Kupp looked slightly sad but otherwise was expressionless. He looked at Ben for several seconds before raising himself one more rung. He was half out of the hatch now, and there he settled.

"So, Ben, what is your little game?"

For a moment Ben thought he was seeing things, that this wasn't Mr Kupp at all. His voice was different, not the muddly, petulant Deputy any more, but something much worse. There was a chilling, calculated calm to his voice that Ben had never heard before. He found he could not speak.

"I must thank you for delivering to the staff room that USB that did not belong to you. But now I must ask you what you know about it. Ben?"

"Everything," Ben managed to say. He knew his voice lacked all conviction.

"Oh, I doubt that, Ben. Tell me, Ben, are you a code cracker?" This delivered with smiling, unmistakable sarcasm. "You see, Ben, my business transactions do not have many names or dates or details on them. And any they do have are completely disguised. All names have been changed, as they say, to protect the innocent. You have no proof of any misdemeanour, and now you do not even have the memory stick. I have that, Ben." Mr Kupp raised himself further out of the hatch until he was standing on the flat leaded roof. He was still looking up at Ben, though. Twenty feet of sloping roof was all that separated them.

Ben breathed deeply and at last found his voice.

"I don't need proof. I know what you are, what you have done."

"Ah, really? And what have I done, Ben?"

You are a drug dealer. You and Danny. You supply the staff too, and..."

"...I was responsible for dear Mr Luxmore's accident? No, innocent of the great offence actually. That was all that oaf Danny's doing. I just wanted the DVD back. We all wanted it. Mr Kretchner, so careless with computers and things. It could have had anything on it. I believe it was quite nasty. So distasteful. But Danny, well, that was me. Like force feeding a goose. What I gave him could have killed a rhinocerous. And lastly, Ben, before I kill you, there is the question of Eleni, isn't there? Sweet girl!"

"You bastard, you fucking bastard! What did you do to her!"

"Nothing, Ben..."

"You damned liar!"

"...I never touched her! She ran from me, Ben, and hid. You see, I knew she had broken into my study and my computer. I suppose the nosy brat had been in Mr Kretchner's room too. I actually just missed her, but the settings had been changed, the window catch was bent. I knew someone had been meddling. So I waited for her."

There was a sudden flurry of sound from the yard below, shouting, more shouting, excited, raised voices.

"You did try to kill her, you bastard, you did! She might still die!"

"She did it to herself herself, Ben. I never touched her." Kupp started up the slope of the roof towards Ben. He kept his eyes fixed on Ben. He seemed sure-footed, but he took it carefully, fixing Ben all the time with his slightly amused expression as if he had come to help rather than kill.

"Enough, Ben, this is the end. Possibly for both of us, but definitely for you. You and your nasty little friends have tried to destroy me, and I cannot allow you to get away with it." Now sitting firmly astride the apex of the roof Kupp raised his hands in a gesture of hopelessness. "A Prep. school, Ben, in the country. What better place could there be to hide a little illicit business, I thought. Well, it seems I was wrong."

Then Ben, suddenly remembering, reached into his pocket. And in his hand were several identical USB sticks. He was beginning to hyperventilate as he experienced terror beyond anything he had ever known. Terror tinged with a strange, paradoxical feeling of triumph and elation.

"Look, Kupp... Kuppcake, you wretched little man. More copies, all full of your crimes, and none for you!" Reaching his arm behind him he flung them over the edge of the roof into the invisible yard below. Kupp reacted immediately moving steadily like some grotesque spider towards the trembling boy.

"No more talk, Ben, your time is over."

And with only feet to go, Ben reached behind him, felt the lightning conductor, pulled at the wooden object fastened between it and the chimney. And as Kupp reached out to grab him Ben, off balance, swung. The baseball bat hit Kupp just above the left knee. Kupp grunted but kept his grip. Ben lifted the bat again, Kupp raised his hands to ward off the blow, and ducked. Ben swung again, and missed almost dislodging himself from his perch. But in avoiding the blow Kupp had thrown his weight onto his injured leg which did not respond. He toppled over and slid slowly down the incline, unable to grip with feet or hands. Ben watched in terrified anticipation. And then Kupp hit the parapet and stopped. Carefully he raised himself until he was in a crouching position, and started up the slope again. It was Ben's last chance. He raised the bat above his head and flung it with all his strength at Kupp's head. But terror and exhaustion had taken their toll and he was again wide of the mark. The bat smashed into the parapet and broke in two. Kupp looked up at Ben, and took the one small step needed to reach the broken handle.

One small step with his left leg, which gave way immediately. And then he was gone. He didn't make a sound as he fell. But those in the yard who saw him fall did.

Ben stayed where he was. He heard the screams from the yard below, he heard the deeper sound of barked orders from voices of authority. Then the noise died as his terrified, appalled, rapidly fragmenting mind turned in on itself and faced the black beast that had been growing there, festering, spreading through his whole body for months, years. He tried to reassess his feelings to understand the enormity of what had just happened but found that he hadn't any feelings to reassess. The person that had been "Ben" had ceased to exist. He had done what he set out to do, and all the battles and confrontations and plotting and scheming were suddenly over. Then his thoughts turned to Eleni. Eleni, the loyal friend, the brave friend, the one who wouldn't give up, the one who was lying desperately ill and damaged in hospital.

Eleni, the one who would never want to speak to him again.

He sat back against the cold stone of the chimney and stared up at the empty, unfeeling sky. He looked round from left to right at the fields and hills, the random copses that were sprinkled over the landscape. It was all indifferent to him, he was not part of it any more. It was there and he was here, and it would always be so from now on. He closed his eyes and his inner voice emerged from the deep shadows of his tortured mind. He pushed his head back hard against the flaking stone behind him and howled at the sun.

32

What surprised him later was the fact that he remembered very clearly how he got back down to the ground.

Carefully and methodically he hitched his way along the roof, slid in a controlled single movement down to the hatch, opened it and started down the ladder closing the hatch and leaving him in almost pitch darkness for a few seconds. The first person he met was Penny, the junior matron, who stood aside for him, merely mouthing his name soundlessly as he passed. Then he heard a rapid succession of footsteps echoing up the main stairwell. He came into view and the footsteps ceased. Matron, in her white coat, was there with Mr Cooper and Miss Garforth. Behind them were the shocked faces of his friends, Leo and Alec, with Amy and Kate, frozen between steps, staring up at him. The darkness of the stairwell yawned invitingly all the way down to the worn stone three floors below. Matron found her voice first.

"Ben, you must come with us," she said, then, inconsequentially, "you see that don't you?" Ben nodded slowly and continued down the stairs. They made way for him and at the foot of the first flight of stairs he walked automatically into the matrons' surgery and sat down on a red plastic chair. It squeaked slightly as his back settled into its moulded shape.

Mr Cooper, Miss Garforth and Matron came in and shut the door behind them. Miss Garforth was red-eyed and trembling. He reached into his pocket and brought out two more USB sticks. He held out his hand and dropped them onto the floor. They were not for him anymore. He sighed and looked out of the window at the thin, high, motionless clouds.

And here I am at the end of it all. I, the instigator. I the crazy one, out of control. Ben, the murderer.

33

Ben got used to the walls quickly.

After two months he'd grown quite accustomed to the smell of new paint, the excess of light pouring through the thickly glazed windows and the slightly grubby but prolific skylights. There were no stairs, but the long corridors and unevenly spaced double doors created a confusion that he had no particular desire to unravel, but by the end of the first year his feet knew every worn carpet tile. Besides, as often as not, all he had to do was obey the command "Follow me, please."

He enjoyed the talks with Dr. Sayle ("Just call me Angela.") and the others. They were more like monologues. They would prompt him with some innocent question ("How are you this morning, Ben?"), and he would start. Their glazed expressions didn't make much difference. It was all being recorded anyway, he knew.

Visits from his mother were more difficult. Her questions were full of incomprehension and became a little monotonous after the third of fourth visit. So Ben stopped talking to her. She would still bring him things, books, and fruit ("I am not an invalid."), but would leave with some muttered excuse after a few minutes.

But it was the letters that kept him going, and he kept them all together in an indexed box, rereading them according to his mood on a particular day. Amy (typical girl!) wrote regularly and was the most loyal correspondent. One particular letter had become quite crumpled and worn.

Dear Ben, (it said)

How are you? Please write when you can. It's nearly a year now since, well, since we left. It's been a good year really and people have stopped pestering me about things (when they do pester me I clam up. Can you picture me not speaking? Probably not). Alec has been here twice but I had to smack him when he started signing autographs for "My adoring fans". But he's just the same. I'm going to Cyprus with him and his family in August.

They won't let me come to see you, Ben. None of us are allowed. They don't understand. They say you need time. We all need that. Eleni needs time too. Have you heard how she is getting on? Signs of improvement, I've heard. Definitely; but no real awareness yet. Eye movements and a few mumbled words, but no recognition yet. I'm sure it's just a matter of time, Ben. There I go again, this time business.

Did you get all the information you wanted from us? Have you finished writing?

How much longer will you be there, Ben? "Indeterminate" they said. So could be a week or a hundred years? Sorry, don't mean to depress you, but what are they doing?

Ben, why did you admit to killing Kupp? Because you didn't. He fell. We know that, but why didn't you say so? It was self defence. You faced up to a problem that none of us could cope with. You are our hero. All that corruption and wickedness swept away, and two of them still locked up! And you of course. But you shouldn't be there.

Anyway, other good news. Mr L played tennis last week. He is in a lovely little cottage near Bridport, and there's a tennis club nearby. He's one of their best players. He and Mrs L are so happy together. I've been to tea there. Oh, yes! You know about Danny's note! Found in a box by his wife last month. As good as a confession, listing all the things he'd done for Kupp – and Kretchner. Admitting he'd just meant to warn Mr L, may be rough him up a bit, but he tried to stop his car, Mr L wouldn't stop so Danny hit him head on. Kupp's orders.

But you've got to get past all that, Ben. Get rid of the ghosts. Forget about that crumbling Stonegate (the golf course and hotel ideas fell through apparently – dry rot inside, wet, outside). Learn to live again, Ben. For Eleni. You said that you loved her. Well prove it. Don't let her go. Think about her. I bet that's what she's doing – thinking about you. Probably what's keeping her going. Think about us too, your friends. Because we all think about you, and talk about you. And miss you. We will be waiting for you when they let you out.

Write to me. Write to me.

Love from Amy XXX

P.S. Alec says "Hi!" and lots of other things that would probably be censored by your brutish guards if I put them in.

P.S.S. Kate says "Hi!" too and "Yaaay!" and "Happy Christmas".

Ben refolded the letter and placed it back in the box. It was the letters that kept him going. Those and the visits from Eleni's parents and Mr and Mrs Luxmore. They didn't try to analyse him, didn't ask him silly questions that he couldn't answer. They just talked to him about Eleni, about Dorset, about life. They never mentioned Stonegate.

But Ben thought about Stonegate. About the good and the bad, about the dreams and the nightmares. Imperceptibly he found himself driving out the bad memories, and more and more often the images he would be left with as he went to sleep would be of the happy times: of Twig in the Vortex and his Kow Klub and of what he had endured in silence, of Chloe sitting on a bookshelf, Leo with his guitar, Poppy and Letty laughing and flirting; the loving couple, Alec and Amy, Biffo and Atlanta and Henry and all the others who had survived the darkness of Stonegate by shining their own bright lights into the shadows. And Eleni, who'd shone brightest of all and almost paid for it with her life.

Epilogue

And I, Ben, hear the door on a sanitized and lonely world close behind me and shut tight. Fresh winds fill my lungs and dissolve five years of mind games and locked doors. The world before me is a green sea of undulating dreams that loses itself on a horizon of cloud-capped whiteness beneath a blue and laughing sky. Swifts scream by in ecstatic ground-skimming arcs in freedoms that only I can share in this spot on a beleaguered and fragile world.

And where to go and what to do? Eighteen years already gone and only a back-pack and a holdall to take me into wild and dangerous future.

I cross the road which is pock-marked with the scars of a million journeys already turned into pasts etched into its bubbling surface. A car, hatch yawning, gobbles my meagre bags greedily. A door stands open. I get in and close it with a soft thud.

Silence. Ten seconds of infinite time slip by as I move from one world to another.

"Shall we go?"

"Yes, Eleni, let's go."

The chains that hold me do not break. They dissolve and are sucked like water into the earth.

The End

About the Author

Peter Erskine was born in Kingston-upon-Thames in 1950. He was educated in private boarding schools in Dorset and Buckinghamshire. After training as a teacher in Cheltenham he spent thirty-eight happy years teaching in three excellent Prep. schools. He loves walking, and did Wainwright's coast-to-coast in 2015. He also loves reading and watching classic and foreign films. He is married, has three children and four grandchildren. He lives in Horsham in West Sussex.

20551994R00151

Printed in Great Britain
by Amazon